NOBODY BUT ARCHIBALD BRAINRIDGE WAS SHY . . .

"I owe you an apology. I oughtn't to have kissed you— especially not here."

"Indeed, I resent being treated like a trollop!"

"Lord, Bella, I'm sorry. It ain't that I don't respect you, but I'm having the devil's own time keeping my hands off you, sweetheart. And you're so curst obstinate, you make it impossible for me to pay my addresses to you properly."

Isabella's eyes flashed. "So I'm to blame, am I?"

"No, you ain't. Not by a long shot. I simply want to say my intentions are honorable and I love you to distraction. More to the point, your jealousy of Fanny gives me hope that you love me."

"Why, you conceited coxcomb! How dare you presume to know my mind?"

"Not your mind, my love, your heart. You love me, Bella. You're just too stubborn to admit it. But make no mistake, I intend to wed you, Isabella Cox, come hell or high water."

ZEBRA'S REGENCY ROMANCES
DAZZLE AND DELIGHT

A BEGUILING INTRIGUE (4441, $3.99)
by Olivia Sumner

Pretty as a picture Justine Riggs cared nothing for propriety. She dressed as a boy, sat on her horse like a jockey, and pondered the stars like a scientist. But when she tried to best the handsome Quenton Fletcher, Marquess of Devon, by proving that she was the better equestrian, he would try to prove Justine's antics were pure folly. The game he had in mind was seduction — never imagining that he might lose his heart in the process!

AN INCONVENIENT ENGAGEMENT (4442, $3.99)
by Joy Reed

Rebecca Wentworth was furious when she saw her betrothed waltzing with another. So she decides to make him jealous by flirting with the handsomest man at the ball, John Collinwood, Earl of Stanford. The "wicked" nobleman knew exactly what the enticing miss was up to — and he was only too happy to play along. But as Rebecca gazed into his magnificent eyes, her errant fiancé was soon utterly forgotten!

SCANDAL'S LADY (4472, $3.99)
by Mary Kingsley

Cassandra was shocked to learn that the new Earl of Lynton was her childhood friend, Nicholas St. John. After years at sea and mixed feelings Nicholas had come home to take the family title. And although Cassandra knew her place as a governess, she could not help the thrill that went through her each time he was near. Nicholas was pleased to find that his old friend Cassandra was his new next door neighbor, but after being near her, he wondered if mere friendship would be enough . . .

HIS LORDSHIP'S REWARD (4473, $3.99)
by Carola Dunn

As the daughter of a seasoned soldier, Fanny Ingram was accustomed to the vagaries of military life and cared not a whit about matters of rank and social standing. So she certainly never foresaw her *tendre* for handsome Viscount Roworth of Kent with whom she was forced to share lodgings, while he carried out his clandestine activities on behalf of the British Army. And though good sense told Roworth to keep his distance, he couldn't stop from taking Fanny in his arms for a kiss that made all hearts equal!

Phylis Warady
The Persistent Suitor

ZEBRA BOOKS
KENSINGTON PUBLISHING CORP.

This book is dedicated to my children: Anne,
April, and Stephen; my sons-in-law: Dennis and
Stephen; and my grandsons: Brian and Kyle.

ZEBRA BOOKS are published by

Kensington Publishing Corp.
850 Third Avenue
New York, NY 10022

First Printing: April, 1995

Printed in the United States of America

One

Archibald Brainridge raised gray eyes from a piece of vellum covered with a spidery, black-inked scrawl, a perplexed expression on his good-natured countenance.

"If that don't beat the Dutch! Godfather orders me up to London to pay him a call."

Percy, his valet, perked his ears. "The earl's getting on, sir. His lordship's in his eighties, I believe."

"What's that to say to anything? Unless you mean to hint he's losing his wits. What can he want? I thought he washed his hands of me five years ago."

"I recall the occasion, sir," Percy admitted dryly as he brushed his young master's pale Brutus-cropped locks.

"By heaven, so do I! What a peal he rang over me!"

"Be that as it may, I think you should go, sir. Obviously your godfather's days are numbered. He may wish to make his peace with you."

"I've ever been fond of the peppery old curmudgeon," Archie admitted grudgingly. He gave a rueful grin. "Unfortunately, I cannot afford to go haring off to London at present. I must put him off."

A quaver in his voice, Percy said hesitantly, "If your pockets are to let, I won't scruple to advance you the price of a seat on the mail coach, sir."

Archie awarded his long-time valet a measured look. Sadly, Percy still regarded him as the feckless fribble he'd been in his salad days. His eyes glittered with mischief as he decided to twit Percy for his lack of perception.

"Why, Percy, you sly dog! Money put by, have you? Where was it two nights past when I needed a little of the ready for dicing?"

The valet bristled. "Do you take me for a fool? While perfectly willing to make you a sensible loan on occasion, I've not the smallest wish to throw good money after bad at a gaming table."

Amused by Percy's show of outraged dignity, Archie's broad shoulders shook with suppressed laughter. "A fool? Perish the thought! I shudder to think what would have become of me without your sterling example."

The valet drew himself up to his full height. "I trust you intend to accept my offer, sir?"

He really shouldn't tease his valet whose

loyalty could not be faulted, Archie reflected. Not when, up until quite recently, the man had often been obliged to wait— sometimes for months— for his wages.

Archie cast Percy a placating smile. "No need to cut up stiff. I'm not under the hatches. Simply put, I can't leave Brainridge Hall until after spring planting."

Percy had the grace to look suitably chagrined. "I beg your pardon, sir. I confess I'd forgotten how seriously you take your responsibilities ever since your father removed to Leicestershire after appointing you his bailiff."

"Gammon! No offense taken, I assure you," averred Archie, his equanimity restored.

Six weeks later, travel-weary from the constant jolts of the public carriage, Archibald Brainridge lifted the doorknocker at the Earl of Chandos's town house.

The earl's aged major domo opened the door and ushered him into the front salon. "Good to see you again, Master Archibald."

Archie peered quizzically at the stately servant, whom he had known since he was in shortcoats. "You're looking fit, Victor. How is my godfather?"

"In something of a pother due to a flare up of the gout. Otherwise in fair health for a man of his years. Do excuse me. His lordship left strict orders he was to be informed the instant you arrived."

Resigned to a wait, Archie recalled the last time he'd set foot inside his godfather's town house. Since Archie's father had been hard pressed to educate three older sons, Chandos had generously assumed the cost of his godson's education. Thus, as a mere stripling of nineteen, sent down from Oxford, Archie had felt obliged to pay his benefactor a call. What a quake the crusty old nobleman had put him in on that occasion, Archie mused. Even now, he could not be entirely easy.

The sound of shuffling footsteps signaling the major domo's imminent reappearance broke his concentration.

"His lordship will receive you now, Master Archibald."

Minutes later, Archie knuckled the bookroom's oak door and entered in response to Chandos's command.

Greeted by a blast of hot air, Archie reeled back then, squaring his shoulders, advanced with a firm step. Though a blazing fire gave off a sweltering heat, the old man sat bundled in a profusion of comforters and quilts. As Archie neared a wing chair covered in red velvet, he recollected that his godfather— in common with the Prince Regent— always felt cold, and consequently kept the rooms he frequented excessively hot.

As he came to a halt, Archie glimpsed the

elderly nobleman's keen black eyes peering up at him. With a shock, he noted how much Chandos had aged during their estrangement.

The octogenarian held out a frail hand. Archie shook it gently.

"Mind you don't jar my curst leg," Chandos admonished.

Archie sympathetically regarded the swollen appendage propped upon a footstool with needlepointed cover. "The gout, sir?"

"Damme yes! Not to mention the dropsy and a touch of dyspepsia," the old man grumbled. "However, I didn't order you up to London to recite a laundry list of my infirmities. Sit down. I've a proposition to make you."

Archie perched gingerly on the edge of a French-styled sofa, squirming a little in reaction to the heat. He loosened his neckcloth, a thing he didn't do usually as it put his valet into a pelter. But what did that signify considering that the humidity was rapidly wilting whatever starch remained?

"Not buckled yet?" Chandos inquired.

"Is that so wonderful, sir? As you know, I've no prospects. The dragon mamas are not at all anxious for me to dangle after their eligible daughters."

"Stuff! You spring from good stock. That should count for something. Wouldn't surprise me—should you make a push—the mamas would soften. Only think, if you manage to charm a female with a respectable fortune, you could settle your debts and start again with a clean slate."

Archie sprang up from the sofa, indignation mirrored on his flushed face. "Sir, I draw the line at becoming a fortune hunter!"

Chandos burst into an appreciative cackle. "Steady there, lad. Didn't mean to vex you."

"No offense taken, sir," Archie said, his stiff demeanor belying his civil response.

"Excellent. Now hold your tongue, lest I lose my thread." His lordship hesitated, then plunged on determinedly. "Since I find myself plagued by all manner of ills, it's high time I set my house in order."

"Oh, but— "

"Do not interrupt!" ordered Chandos, bestowing a heavy scowl upon his godson. Satisfied he had silenced Archie at last, Chandos continued in a softer vein, "Having neither chick nor child of my own, I fear I dealt with you too harshly when you were sent down from Oxford for a mere schoolboy's prank."

Faintly embarrassed by the unexpected whitewashing of his character, Archie tugged once again at his neckcloth. Never had he suspected how difficult it could be to keep his tongue between his teeth.

"To make amends for my shabby treatment," the old man rasped, "I propose to settle your debts and make you a modest allowance, provided you promise to steer clear of all wagering for a period of one year. What do you say to that, my boy?"

"You are too kind by half, sir. However, I'm not sure I should accept. At four and twenty, it's time I solved my own problems without outside assistance."

"Pray don't allow pride to get in the way of common sense. There's no disgrace in accepting my terms, provided you strive to uphold your part of the bargain."

Godfather had a point, Archie conceded. While he was safe enough buried in Herfordshire, London was a different kettle of fish. Suffice to say, that if his creditors got wind of his presence, he'd be hounded to death. Still, he refused to be less than candid.

"Even so, it would be remiss of me if I failed to make known to you that the sum total of my debts is truly monstrous. Perhaps you should have your man of business—"

"Do you take me for a slowtop?" Chandos railed. "My solicitor has already looked into the matter. Well, Archibald, what is your answer to my proposition?"

Archie smiled faintly. "I accept of course. Only a sapskull would refuse such a handsome offer."

"Capital! I'll have your hand on it."

Archie stood and clasped the proffered

frail hand, mindful not to crush it in his stronger grip.

"Make no mistake!" his lordship warned. "Should it come to my ears you've slipped back to gaming, I intend to call you to book."

"You have my word I won't, sir. However, if I somehow make a mull of it, I'd like to think I've the bottom to tell you so to your face."

"Lobcock! Even as a green hafling, your honor was never in question."

"Kind of you to say so, sir."

Chandos dismissed Archie's perfunctory bow with an impatient wave of his bony hand. "On to my second proposal. A bit more difficult to bring off, I will own, but greatly to your advantage if you come up to scratch. Not to mince words, if you manage to persuade some eligible female to marry you, I'll make you heir to my fortune when I pass on. Mind, you must promise not to breathe a word of our arrangement to your intended."

Archie's brow puckered. "Am I to understand, my lord, that my bride must command a fortune of her own?"

"By no means. I don't care if she has tuppence. Only that she remain ignorant of your improved prospects until after the ceremony. One reason I never married is I didn't wish to risk the mortification of discovering

I was shackled to some grasping female," Chandos grumbled. "Take my fortune and welcome I say, provided you keep your lips sealed until you've convinced some eligible young miss to accept you solely on the strength of your lineage and reformed character."

"I understand, sir, though heaven knows, since I'm acquainted with precious few young ladies at present, what you ask won't be easy."

Yet, even as he spoke, Archie's thoughts turned to his childhood friend, Isabella Cox. His troubled countenance brightened. If he took advantage of his godfather's generosity, he'd be in a position to rescue her from a life of penury.

"Where's your pluck, Godson? What do you stand to lose? In order to ease your way, I'll stake you to some new clothes. So even if you fail to discover someone who will look deep enough to see more in you than the size of your purse, you'll still come out ahead. Your debts will be settled. You'll have an adequate allowance and be rigged out in the first stare of fashion."

"Very well, sir, I'll do my best." Once again Archie carefully shook the old man's hand.

"That's settled then." Chandos heaved a relieved sigh. "You'll have to hang about town at least a fortnight so the Bond Street tailors can run you up a decent suit, which judging from the cut of your coat, you stand badly in need of. Come to think of it, make free of my town house whenever you're in London. I imagine you will wish to take in the season."

"Mayhap, I will, sir, and thank you for—"

"Gammon! Out of my sight, before I change my mind. I'll wager you could do with a hot bath and a change of linen after your rackety trip."

Archie chuckled. "You've the right of it, sir. Indeed, what else is to be expected when one travels by mail coach?" With a respectful bow to the cantankerous old man, he left the overheated bookroom.

"Fustian!" exclaimed Miss Isabella Cox.

Sensibilities outraged, she regarded Archie through veiled lashes. Inexplicably, indignation gave way to admiration when she noticed that the cut of his elegant new coat made his shoulders seem broader. Indeed, she had never seen him looking so handsome. She pressed her hand over her heart. Never had it fluttered so erratically before this moment. Disturbed by emotions she didn't understand, she averted her gaze.

Unhappily, her eyes came to rest upon the hem of her gown— a gown she'd been obliged to lengthen. Isabella stared at the ugly line demarking the unfaded material of the let-down hem from the rest of her gown. The contrast between Archie, looking for once as fine as sixpence, and her own shabby appearance triggered a fresh spurt of anger.

Archie quelled a shiver. Despite his befuddled state, he was all but certain Isabella's sapphire-blue eyes seethed with resentment. Clearly she was overset. Why else would she be twisting her handkerchief?

"You're making a cake of yourself, Archie. Climb up off your knees, do!"

"Gladly, Bella, after I've finished making you an offer." Beaming benevolently, he blinked in the vain hope of keeping her face in focus.

Unfortunately, when he'd jogged past the Rose and Crown on his piebald, Archie had been besieged by icy fingers of doubt and had felt a burning need to bolster his sagging spirits with a little Dutch courage. Thus he'd entered the taproom and ordered a tankard. One had led to two. Two had led to three.

Now, gazing at Bella's blurred image, Archie silently acknowledged the minx had matured into a comely female. Indeed, he regretted that their paths had seldom crossed since her return to Cox Manor from a young ladies' seminary. The fact that they had seen so little of each other was as much his fault as hers, he freely admitted. Ever since he'd squandered the small sum bequeathed to him by his mother, he'd pointedly avoided all females . . . whenever possible. Nonetheless, when Isabella's father died recently leaving her penniless, it had saddened him that he lacked the power to help her come about. But now, thanks to his godfather's change of heart, he was in a position to make her an offer. Too bad Isabella did not seem at all impressed by his magnanimous gesture. On the contrary, her scowl radiated disapproval. In vain, Archie scoured his brain in search of something he'd done to put himself in her bad books.

Perhaps the grudge she nursed dated back to their childhood. As a lad, he had barely tolerated the little hoyden who'd trailed after him on her Shetland pony, whenever he rode his frisky mount. Yet, what else had she expected, considering she was six years his junior and a female to boot!

Archie braved a furtive glance into Isabella's stormy countenance. The chill rising from the stone floor, passing through the threadbare Turkey carpet and seeping into his shin bones, was nothing compared to her icy stare.

"Archibald Brainridge, you're foxed!" She stamped her slippered foot. "Furthermore, I'd thank you not to tease me. I've no time for nonsense."

"Tease you? No such thing. Bella, I'm in earnest. Why else would I be at your feet?"

"In earnest? Pray, sir, have done."

"Not until you give me your answer."

Isabella gave an exasperated sigh. "Oh very well!" she capitulated with ill grace. "Sir, I am aware of the *honor* you do me, but I cannot accept your *flattering* offer." A healthy swath of sarcasm had crept into her voice. "Now if you will kindly excuse me, I must speak to Ned."

"Pray don't be so hasty, Bella. Do take a moment to consider your straitened circumstances."

"Rest assured, I already have," she responded sweetly. "I mean to procure a post as a lady's companion."

Archie's fair skin reddened alarmingly. "Confound it, Bella, such a post will lower your social standing— to say nothing of your prospects."

Isabella stiffened. "In the marriage mart, you mean? Since I've no dowry, my expectations in that quarter were never very high."

"Your father *would* squander money set aside for that purpose at the gaming tables! But it don't signify. I don't care whether you've a button to your name. If you need more time to consider my offer— "

"More time?" she interrupted. "Sir, I beg leave to tell you I know my own mind. I won't marry a gamester! Why, we don't have a groat between us. Wherever did you get such a crack-brained idea?"

Clearly his business with Isabella was not going well, Archie ruefully conceded. As his head began to clear, the specter of his god-father's prune-wizened countenance rushed to the foreground of his consciousness.

Slightly desperate now, he coaxed, "I beg you to reconsider."

"Indeed, I will not! What a kickup there'll be if your father gets wind of this!"

"What has he to say about it? I'll be five-and-twenty in a few months."

But a moment's reflection forced Archie to admit she was right. Should Isabella accept his offer, he doubted his father would be best pleased.

Sent down from Oxford, Archie had got in thick with Bella's father. As a result, the younger man developed imprudent habits, such as wagering money he could ill afford on cock fights or cards and quaffing ale by the jugful at the Rose and Crown. Consequently, Archie's father had long since laid the blame for his youngest son's dis-solute behavior upon Sir Reginald Cox's doorstep.

Archie shifted his weight on his cold, stiff knees. Because of innovative practices he'd introduced as the bailiff at Brainridge Hall during the past year, he hoped he had earned a modicum of grudging respect from his father. But even if he were mistaken in this assumption, his father's opinion no longer mattered. Thanks to Chandos's generosity, Archie had a chance to start fresh— if only Bella could be made to look favorably on his suit.

He frowned. What a devilish fix! He'd had such high hopes when he'd set out from Brainridge Hall all rigged out in a new coat by Weston and pale yellow breeches. Percy had taken pains to polish his master's Hessians until he could see his reflection in them and had arranged Archie's neckcloth to perfection. If only Archie's avoidance of the female gender hadn't resulted in him feeling so shy in their presence.

Sober now, but still kneeling on the stone-cold drawing room floor, Archie was forced to admit he had only himself to blame. He'd insulted Isabella by making his offer while foxed. Obviously, his shameful rag-manners had given her a disgust of him. Lord, what a mull he'd made of it!

Archie's warm gray eyes anxiously scanned Isabella's heart-shaped face, hoping against hope that her attitude would soften. After all, if he must get leg-shackled, he preferred it to be to someone he'd been fond of since he was in shortcoats.

"Am I to understand, Bella, that you are rejecting my proposal?"

"Of all the shabby, hare-brained offers! I wouldn't marry you, Archibald Brainridge, for all the tea in China!"

Two

Overset, Isabella ran from the parlor with unladylike haste. Midway up circular stairs, she tripped and just managed to catch hold of the banister before she took a tumble. A furtive backward glance revealed her besotted suitor eying her indecorous retreat, his broad forehead puckered in perplexity. Turning, she scrambled up the remaining steps, not halting to catch her breath until she reached her bedchamber.

Usually the room's airy charm served as a cool balm whenever she was agitated, but not today. On the contrary, her seething emotions blinded her to the pale-blue wallpaper overprinted in white daisies with bright yellow centers.

Nerves ashamble, she cast off her dove gray dress with its frayed cuffs and turned down hem and shrugged into a riding habit of bronze twill. Beautifully, if simply, cut, it had languished in a trunk until she had rescued it. Indeed, the habit had been her mother's, a lady Isabella had no memory of since Lady Cox had died in childbirth.

As she picked up her riding crop, Isabella's thoughts returned to Archibald Brainridge. How abysmally lowering to realize he had felt it necessary to stoke up his resolve with drink before he could come up to scratch, especially since his proposal was very likely the only offer she would ever get. Isabella winced. Then, determined to shake off her depression, she straightened her spine and walked briskly from the room.

But, despite her resolve, the memory of her childhood idol weaving unsteadily on bent knees made her cheeks burn as she descended the stairs. She halted at the foot to give herself a chance to peruse the reception hall, as always cast in gloomy shadow due to a regrettable lack of windows. If possible, she wished to avoid a second encounter with her foxed suitor. Convinced she would be tempting fate if she tried to sneak past the sitting room on her way to the back door, she left the manor through the front entrance.

Isabella picked her way along the unkempt path, skirting tall weeds that had sprung up on the seldom-used route, ducking to dodge overlong branches of untamed shrubbery. As she neared the stable yard her keen eyes scanned the scene.

The fact that Archie's piebald was no longer tethered to the hitching post triggered a sigh of relief. Thank goodness she needn't tease herself with the unsettling prospect of blundering into another embarrassing encounter.

Entering the stable, she called for Ned. Unable to run the groom to ground, she slung a saddle across the back of a frisky mare, dubbed Starlight by Isabella's father. The thoroughbred had been much prized by the deceased gamester, who'd never stinted on horseflesh— no matter that the manor's roof leaked or that the entire estate fell into shambles.

Disdaining the saddle slapped upon her back, the horse reared, forcing Isabella to devote precious moments coaxing the skittish mount to stand quiet.

Isabella stroked Starlight's forelock. "Steady, girl. What you and I need to settle us down is a good gallop."

Once mounted, she gave a rueful laugh. If her father could see her seated upon his prized mare, he would have a royal fit. She kept her fidgety mount on short rein until they reached an open meadow where she gave Starlight her head, reveling in the ensuing cantor. At last, the horse slackened her pace. Wishing to ride alongside the winding stream, Isabella urged her mount into the woods. During their ramble, she mulled over

Archibald Brainridge's unexpected offer. What maggot had invaded the amiable scapegrace's upper story?

Had his father suggested Archie propose? No, she thought not. If that gentleman had decided to drop a hint in his youngest offspring's ear, it would be to suggest that he dangle after some female commanding a handsome dowry.

The mere thought of the dismal future she faced made her shiver. The estate was entailed—the only reason her father hadn't wagered it away. It would pass to a distant male relative, whom she expected to arrive any day.

As to Archie, the more she ruminated about his offer, the more she was inclined to attribute it to a burst of misguided chivalry. In a way, she regretted she could not seriously consider his proposal. If truth be told, he'd been the object of a childhood *tendre* from which she'd never quite recovered. Even so, she wasn't such a widgeon that she'd agree to throw in with a wastrel.

Not that Archie didn't have many good traits of character that somewhat offset his predilection to gaming. Isabella's expression softened as she remembered his gentleness when he'd broken the news to her of her father's death.

Apparently, when the Rose and Crown closed its taproom, Sir Reginald had set out for home, inebriated. En route, he'd taken a notion of making Starlight jump a steep stone wall. The stout mare had cleared it, but Isabella's father had lost his seat and gone flying up into the air, his head striking the wall on his way down.

Archie, who'd accompanied Sir Reginald on the fatal ride, had been a great comfort to her on that sad occasion. Nevertheless, it would never do to accept his suit. As disagreeable as it was to be obliged to earn her keep, at least her life would be more orderly than it had been under her father's roof. That is, it would be if she managed to find a post as a lady's companion.

Isabella frowned. If only Aunt Hermione would answer her letter— preferably before she was turned out of Cox Manor by the new heir. Her expression grew pensive. The air of mystery surrounding her father's only sister never failed to intrigue her. Judging from bits of past history she'd managed to glean, she had to assume Aunt Hermione was a trifle eccentric.

Now that she didn't have cause to be grateful to the Ponsonbys, Isabella mused. Indeed, shortly before her fifteenth birthday, her aunt's husband, Lord Ponsonby, had arrived uninvited at Cox Manor. Sir Reginald's welcome had been grudging to say the least.

Isabella was under the impression they'd

quarreled about her future, though she'd never managed to get the truth sorted out to her complete satisfaction. Nor, thanks to her uncle's reticence, had she been able to learn anything substantial about her aunt. All she knew was, though Aunt Hermione had been judged an Incomparable during her come-out, two years after her marriage she had retired to her husband's Irish estate, where she had become something of a recluse.

Isabella broke into a smile. The result of Lord Ponsonby's visit had been a happy one in her case. Uncle Robert had insisted upon bearing the cost of having her bedchamber refurbished. Furthermore, he'd engaged a local seamstress to make Isabella several gowns. On top of that, he had arranged for her to attend a fashionable ladies' seminary. While there, from time to time, Isabella had received pin money, and, more rarely, a brief note from her aunt, inquiring about her niece's progress.

Frowning slightly, Isabella nudged the mare in the direction of the manor. She'd completed her studies at the seminary near the end of her seventeenth year. Shortly after her return to Cox Manor, she had received a curt missive in her aunt's graceful hand informing her of her uncle's death. But though she had promptly penned her condolences, she had received no further correspondence from her aunt. Not even on her eighteenth birthday, though in the past she had received a small gift and a silver crown to mark the anniversary.

Isabella sighed. How she would miss her daily gallop once she left Cox Manor. If only Aunt Hermione would write and offer her niece a place to stay until she could find a suitable position.

Disheartened, Isabella urged the mare into the stable yard.

Ned shambled forward to help her alight. "Did her give you any trouble, miss?"

"Starlight? Not at all. All she needed to improve her spirits was a brisk run."

Ned's eyes flicked toward the manor. "The new heir has come."

For the first time she noticed the travel-stained carriage standing in the yard. Isabella's chest ached as if a sudden blow had knocked the wind from her lungs. "My cousin is finally here?"

"Aye, miss. Just finished rubbing down a pair of the sorriest horseflesh I ever seed. Ordered me to wash down his coach next. But don't you worrit. I'll tend to Starlight first," the groom promised as he took the reins.

"What's he like, Ned?"

He snorted. "Stiff as a poker— with manners to match. Told him you wuz off on your morning ride. Didn't like it above half.''

"How disagreeable to be sure!"

Her hands flew to her hair in a futile attempt to comb stray blond tendrils back into line. "I must slip up to my room and change."

"Afore you go, I've a bit of the ready put by in a sock. If you ever be in need of it, just ask."

"Why Ned, how dear of you." She awarded him a warm smile. "Rest assured I shall remember to apply to you, should I find myself in need of a loan."

Beaming shyly, the groom gave a tug on the mare's reins and began to lead her away.

"Wait Ned."

The groom halted.

"After you've given Starlight a rubdown, come round to the scullery, if you please. I desire to send a note to the parsonage asking Miss Finch to play chaperone at Cox Manor for a time."

"Aye, miss."

Isabella hurried along the path. How fortunate the vicar had a tiresomely prim and proper older sister. With Miss Finch in residence, no one was likely to raise a single eyebrow. It wouldn't do to give the local gabblemongers any excuse to gossip.

Unless the new heir planned to board at the Rose and Crown until she quit the manor?

In that event, she'd have no need of the vicar's sister. No, Isabella decided, her cousin planned to stay at Cox Manor. Otherwise, he wouldn't have ordered Ned to unharness his team and wash his coach.

Entering the scullery, she searched through the drawers until she found a piece of writing paper. Dipping quill into inkbottle, she dashed off a hasty note to Miss Finch, which she left in plain sight for Ned. Next, she pulled off her riding boots and set them beside the back door, hoping to slip quietly up to her room in order to make herself presentable before she met the new heir.

Isabella was halfway up the circular staircase when a falsetto voice rang out. "Ah, there you are, cousin. Back from your morning ride I see. Come down, coz, and allow me to make your acquaintance."

Acutely aware of her hot, dusty face and tangled hair, Isabella reluctantly descended, studying the tall, painfully thin man as she narrowed the distance between them. About thirty, attired in black, with the exception of his white shirt and neckcloth, he claimed both her hands the instant she reached the foot of the stairs.

Ned's description of him was so apt, Isabella was obliged to choke back a giggle. Not only poker-faced, but poker-backed as well. In truth, he held himself so stiffly upright she questioned whether it was within his power to bend or sit. Top lofty! she decided as she dropped a curtsy.

"Cousin Gerald Cox, I presume?"

"At your service, ma'am."

He could bend after all, she conceded as she watched him straighten from his bow.

"I hope you won't take it amiss, but I am now Sir Gerald. You'll find I'm a high stickler for the proprieties. A pity your father succumbed in his prime. May I offer my condolences."

"Thank you, Sir Gerald," she said demurely.

"I daresay I may be a bit beforehand in light of your recent bereavement," his thin voice piped. "Nonetheless, since you are without a proper chaperone, I feel I must speak out at once in order to guard your reputation. In short, Cousin Isabella, will you do me the honor of becoming my wife?"

Isabella reeled back. Such presumption, she thought. Especially since she had never laid eyes on the man before in her life. Her initial amazement was swiftly superseded by cynicism. What bouncers he told! Should she accept his offer, he would not feel honored. On the contrary, he would think he was doing her a favor.

Apparently misinterpreting her silence for awe, Sir Gerald prattled on. "The banns can be read in church on Sunday three days hence, as well as the next two Sabbaths, with the ceremony performed shortly thereafter. In view of your penniless state, I will be most happy to stand the cost of having a wedding dress made up by the local seamstress, provided she can manage on such short notice." He gestured expansively. "I have such plans for the manor, coz, which I fear has fallen in sad disarray."

"Begging your pardon, Sir Gerald—"

"Cousin Gerald," he corrected. "And once we are wed, Gerald." He beamed benignly.

Isabella hid a smirk behind her hand. She wished the conceited coxcomb would make up his mind as to which form of address he preferred.

"Cousin Gerald, I fear I cannot accept your generous offer," she informed him. "As to a chaperone, Miss Finch, the vicar's sister, will be joining us directly. Under the circumstances, I believe she can be persuaded to stay on until I can make suitable arrangements for my future. So, you see, there is no need for you to go to such lengths to protect my reputation."

Sir Gerald stiffened to an even greater degree, a thing Isabella would have believed impossible if she hadn't seen it with her own eyes.

"I trust I haven't offended you by speaking too soon. It is possible," he allowed in a burst of generosity, "that you've already formed a serious attachment."

"Without a dowry that's not very likely, is it?" she asked, with a trace of wistfulness swiftly suppressed. "If you please, cousin, as it's almost noon, may we postpone this conversation until nuncheon? I feel untidy after my morning ramble and beg to be excused to change my dress."

For a moment he looked miffed, then his elongated countenance cleared. "As you wish, cousin." Somehow he managed to negotiate another deep bow.

As she climbed the stairs, his thin voice dogged her footsteps. "You're probably overset. After all it's not everyday that a dowerless maid receives such a handsome offer."

Eyes dancing, Isabella rushed up the remaining stairs, fearful she might laugh out loud. However, she managed to reach the privacy of her bedchamber before falling into the whoops.

Once her laughter had ebbed, she went to stand before her boudoir mirror. She studied her out-of-mode riding habit and wind-tossed hair.

An impish grin lit her dusty face. "Ravishing creature! Guineas to gooseberries, you're the only female in all of England to bring two gentlemen up to scratch in a single morning."

Isabella gave a small, discouraged sigh. "One a besotted gamester; the other a pompous ass!"

Three

At daybreak a week later, Isabella tiptoed along the dimly-lit hall to a bedchamber door. There, she left a note, apologizing for her abrupt departure and thanking Miss Finch for assuming the role of chaperone on such short notice. Then, riding boots in one hand, portmanteau in the other, Isabella crept down the stairs. In stockinged feet, she padded across the reception hall, passed through the gallery and into the kitchen. Praying she wouldn't wake the cook, who was a light sleeper, Isabella stealthily drank a glass of milk and downed two muffins.

She slipped out the back door, taking care it didn't slam. After a short pause to pull on her boots, she wended her way through a weed-filled kitchen garden.

The interior of the stable was dimly lit. Hearing the rustle of straw overhead, she glanced up in time to watch Ned scramble down a ladder from the loft.

"Wot brings you from your warm bed

afore the sun's up proper, miss?" he asked, rubbing his eyes with his knuckles.

"Sorry to wake you, but I mean to catch the mail coach bound for London this morning. That is, I plan to if you'll lend me the money in your sock."

"You be welcome to it. I'll fetch it afore I saddle the mare."

While the groom rescaled the ladder, Isabella approached Starlight's stall. "Good morning, beauty. Here's a treat for you." She fed the mare a lump of sugar filched from the pantry.

Ned rejoined her, bridle in hand. Expression pensive, he slipped it over Starlight's head, patting her fondly before adjusting the bit. "Look you, miss. Should you fall on hard times, you could do with a nest egg. This mare be a prime piece of horseflesh. I've a mind to take her to Newmarket where her will fetch top price."

Isabella's spirits rose. "What a capital notion! I quite forgot Starlight's not part of the entailment. How soon can you leave?"

The groom's tanned sinewy hands tightened the saddle girth. "I've a mind to collect the mare from the inn's stable and continue on me way after you board the mail coach."

"Excellent!" Isabella handed him a folded scrap of paper. "I'll be staying with my aunt in London. Here's her direction."

"Thankee, miss." Ned tucked it into his belt. "Here, let me give you a leg up."

Isabella placed her foot in the cradle he formed with his hands and swung up into the sidesaddle. She held Starlight in check while Ned lashed her portmanteau behind her.

When he handed over a small bag of coins, Isabella was suddenly assailed by a wave of nostalgia. Ned had taught her to ride her first pony. She swallowed the lump in her throat.

"Thanks for the loan. When you sell Starlight, deduct the amount I owe you and send me the rest. And . . . thanks also for ever being my friend. I . . . shall miss you."

"This be no time to play the prattlebox," he admonished. "Off with you afore your prosy cousin wakes."

"If he does, he'll assume I'm off on my usual morning ramble."

"So you hope. Still it don't pay to be too cocky."

"I suppose not," she conceded as she flicked the reins.

Jogging along the dusty road, Isabella kept the mare to a steady trot. Although she faced a two hour wait before the London mail departed from the Rose and Crown, she felt it prudent to leave Cox Manor while Sir Gerald was still abed.

She grimaced. Her cousin would be

shocked by her plan to travel to London in a public coach. She could just imagine the pious lectures he'd feel duty-bound to deliver— should he catch up with her. Isabella urged the mare to a quicker pace.

Minutes later, the Rose and Crown came into view. Isabella dismounted in the stable yard. Misty-eyed, she bid Starlight a fond farewell. She tipped the ostler generously in exchange for his pledge to deny having seen her— should her cousin inquire. Then, charging the ostler to take proper care of the mare until Ned showed up to claim her, Isabella made for the inn carrying her port-manteau.

Inside the Rose and Crown, the innkeeper greeted her with a deferential bow. "Servant, Miss Cox. How may I serve you?"

"I wish to purchase a seat on the London-bound mail coach," she said. "Is it running on schedule?"

"Coachman prides himself on being punctual. Folks hereabouts set their clocks by the horn he toots as rolls into yard."

"Excellent. I'd like to purchase an inside seat."

"You're in luck. Only one left. It's two pounds six."

Isabella paid him, then ticket in hand, said, "I must change into something more suitable for travel. Do you have a room I might retire to?"

"Let me think. The front suite at the top of the stairs is engaged by four young blades bound for the races. However, I do have a small back bedchamber available."

"It will do. How much?"

"Six shillings."

She counted the money into his open palm. "By the by, should my cousin inquire, I'd appreciate it if you'd deny having seen me. Indeed, I'd be happy to make it worth your while."

"No need. I'll keep me gab shut. We was that fond of Sir Reginald hereabouts."

Too fond by half! Isabella thought. But she was being unfair. After all, her father's self-destructive streak wasn't the proprietor's fault.

"Indeed, he always spoke highly of your establishment."

That her ironic tone was quite lost on the innkeeper caused Isabella's smile to linger as she climbed the stairs.

Impatient with the Rose and Crown's lackadaisical service, Malcolm Grandison emerged from the inn's private parlor. The hair on his head and neatly-trimmed Vandyke was black as coal, but touched with silver at his temples and at the tips of his beard.

"Faith, mon, where's the meal I ordered?"

Bowing and scraping, the proprietor promised to see what was holding things up in the kitchen. Time on his hands, Grandison decided to make a short visit to the stable. A tall, well-set-up man in his prime, he reached his destination by a series of long, purposeful strides.

Once inside, he was pleased to find the string of Irish thoroughbreds he was transporting to Newmarket had been expertly rubbed down and were presently being fed and watered.

He broke his stride before Starlight's stall. There, Archie, who'd taken temporary leave of his card playing friends in order to stretch his legs, stood petting the mare.

"Excellent conformation," observed Grandison.

"Quite."

"Your horse?"

Archie's grin was rueful. "Don't I wish. No, this beauty belongs to a neighbor. Are the thoroughbreds yours?"

"For the moment. I plan to sell the lot at Newmarket."

"By jove, my party's bound there as well." He thrust out his hand. "Archibald Brainridge."

Smiling, the Irishman shook it. "Malcolm Grandison. In that case, I'll see you at the track."

"I doubt it, sir. While my friends plan to stay for the races, I've business in Norfolk."

"Pity. We might have become better acquainted."

"That I regret. However, I'm not about to pass up an invitation to visit Coke's farm."

"If you are speaking of Thomas William Coke, the famous agricultural reformer, I can't say I blame you. Are you?"

At Mr. Brainridge's nod, Grandison's assessment of the young man rose several notches. "I take it you're interested in innovative farming methods."

"Avidly, sir. Improved stock breeding as well. You see, my father recently inherited property in Leicester from a distant cousin and when he removed there, he appointed me bailiff of a local property that's been in the family for countless generations. The minute I took over I wrote Mr. Coke. Indeed, his advice has been invaluable."

"Splendid. I imagine your father is busting with pride?"

Mr. Brainridge shrugged. "As to that, I really couldn't say."

Grandison imagined the answer came from the young man's desire not to air his family's dirty linen in public. Mr. Brainridge then expressed his regret that he wouldn't be seeing as much of Grandison at Newmarket as he would like and excused himself.

Mr. Brainridge's retreating footsteps resounding in his ears, Grandison walked past a long row of stalls, not halting until he came to the box that held a magnificent roan stallion.

The horse had sustained a bruised shin-bone while aboard the freighter crossing from Dublin to Holyhead. Grandison's dark blue eyes registered sympathetic concern as he gently patted the horse's right foreleg, from knee to fetlock.

He smiled, pleased most of the soreness had abated. However, by the time he straightened, his expression had turned glum and his eyes held a mutinous expression.

A year ago his partner in the Irish stud farm had died. At first, Rob's widow had been too grief-stricken to take the least interest in the business. But recently she'd demanded a cash settlement for her half share. He'd tried to explain that to sell in haste was imprudent, but her ladyship had remained adamant. The devil! He didn't wish to sell the thoroughbreds. Yet, he had no other choice.

Back at the Rose and Crown, Grandison's brown study persisted throughout the indifferent repast the barmaid set before him. Indeed, by the time she removed the covers and provided him with a fresh bumper of ale, he felt sorely oppressed.

Faith, how was he to guess that a proposal of marriage would throw his partner's widow into a state of panic? Since Rob's death, Lady Ponsonby had come to rely on him more and more. Granted, it was a mistake on his part to emphasize the business advantages of such a union—but, at the time, he had felt what her ladyship craved was security. Consequently, that is what he had offered.

How would she have responded if he had confessed his love for her instead? he wondered. Grandison gave a derisive snort. She would have laughed in his face. Nor could he blame her. For although he had loved Hermione ever since Rob brought her to Ireland as a young bride, ironically, he'd guarded his secret passion all too well. For eighteen years, he'd cultivated a cool, aloof manner toward her—lest she guess his deep regard.

Grandison pinched the bridge of his nose. That Hermione had scorned his marriage offer was bad enough. Far worse, she'd bolted to London. No question he'd rushed his fences like the veriest greenhorn. As a result, the love of his life was in danger of committing a grave social blunder that might well end in her disgrace.

Shaken by the black picture he had painted in his mind, Grandison pounded the table with his fist. No, begorra! Once he had sold the prime string of horseflesh to the highest bidder, he would hie up to town. Mayhap, he would succeed in changing her ladyship's mind before disaster struck. Even if he did not, at least he would be on hand to offer her solace and protection— should she stand in need of either.

Whilst Grandison, inside the inn's private parlor, ruminated on his ill-fated love affair upstairs, in a cramped back bedchamber, Isabella scrambled out of her riding habit and into a slate blue dress of woven gabardine, thankfully not too wrinkled despite her hasty packing. She slipped her feet into sturdy walking shoes and set out black gloves and a black straw bonnet, its brim a bit crushed as a result of being jammed haphazardly into her portmanteau.

She stared dubiously at the riding boots and bronze riding habit. Impossible to squeeze the boots into her portmanteau. In any case, she would have no use for them once she assumed the role of lady's companion. After fretting several minutes, she rolled the habit into a bundle and shoved it, along with the boots, beneath the bed.

A final task remained. She removed the bag of coins Ned had lent her from her reticule. Loosening its drawstring, she emptied the leather purse, arranging the coins in stacks which she counted twice. Next, she calculated the sum needed to buy meals on the way to London, adding a little extra to take care of unforseen expenses, and placed it in her reticule. The rest of the coins she returned to the drawstring pouch which she stuffed inside her portmanteau. There! Now she felt less in danger of attracting a pickpocket each time she opened her reticule.

The knock on the door startled her. Mercy! With less than an hour before the mail coach was due to depart, it would be just like her pompous cousin to run her to ground.

"Archie," she cried in relief, once she'd worked up the courage to open the door. "However did you find me?"

"Spotted Starlight in the stable. Browbeat the innkeeper until he told me where he'd put you."

"That snitcher!" she fumed.

"No need to take a pet. Assure you I won't tell a soul."

"It's not you I'm worried about. It's the innkeeper," she confided, nibbling her lower lip. "If he reveals my whereabouts to my cousin, I'm dished."

"You don't fancy the new heir?"

"I cannot abide him. I hope to board the mail coach before he tracks me down."

Archie sobered. "My dear, you worry me. What shall you do if you don't find a position before your funds dwindle to nothing? Don't go, Bella. Marry me instead."

Discomfited, she shook her head.

He sighed. "No doubt you still hold my ragmannered proposal against me."

"No such thing. I simply don't wish to marry a gamester."

"Not even if I give you my solemn word I won't gamble?"

"Save your breath. Even if I believed you, neither of us has any prospects."

"Stubborn minx," he grumbled. "What will it take to change your mind, I wonder?"

"Give over, Archie. Why won't you take no for an answer?" she asked, exasperation creeping into her voice.

An odd light shone in his gray eyes. "Because you suit me, Bella. No need to look so troubled. I'm willing to give you time to get used to the idea."

The fervor in his voice thrilled Isabella. Yet, it would be foolish to encourage him. She tied on her bonnet and tugged on its brim.

"No need to worry that I'll starve in the streets. I received a letter from my aunt, Lady Ponsonby, inviting me to join her in Berkeley Square. I'll stay with her until I secure a suitable post."

"Since you're set on going, best leave by the back stairs, Bella."

"I plan to," she said stoutly.

"I'll be off then. Goodbye, my dear."

Before she realized what he was about, he had planted a light kiss on her startled mouth. Isabella's lips still throbbed as he slipped from the room. Surely Archie's kiss wasn't the reason she felt so jittery, she mused. The tense muscles in her face relaxed. Of course it was not. The prospect of joining her aunt in town was the reason she was on edge, she told herself firmly.

Archie paused on the upper landing. He had been on the verge of rejoining his cronies when a thin falsetto voice caught his attention. He peered down the stairs at the beleaguered innkeeper being grilled by a tall, stiff-necked gentleman. Bella's cousin, he'd lay odds. Descending, he deliberately interrupted to introduce himself. The innkeeper flashed Archie a grateful smile and slunk off.

"Your property runs parallel to the Brainridge estate. Makes us neighbors," said Archie.

"Then you must know my cousin, Isabella? Have you seen her hereabouts, Brainridge?"

"Shall we discuss the matter over a pitcher of ale?"

"Thank you, no. I never touch spirits."

Curst slowtop! Archie thought, careful to keep a genial smile plastered on his face. No wonder Bella can't stand him. Imagine classing a harmless tankard of ale with the more lethal brews.

"Coffee then?"

"Very well."

"Excellent. Be a good fellow and get us a table, while I place our order."

Three quarters of an hour later, Sir Gerald Cox, having consumed several cups of coffee, swayed in his chair.

"Brew a trifle too strong for you?" Archie asked, his solicitous tone belied by the knowing glint in his eye.

Cox gave a loud belch. "On the contrary, 's best coffee I ever drunk."

Archie grinned. Thanks to the liberal amounts of brandy he had poured into his guest's cup whenever he had succeeded in diverting Sir Gerald's attention, the baronet was beginning to slur his words.

Both men nearly fell off their chairs at the sound of the tin horn signaling the mail coach's imminent departure. Hearing the blast as she reached the foot of the back stairs, Isabella gave a cry of alarm.

She hurried out the kitchen door and raced round the inn, more pleased than she could say to find the Royal Mail Express waiting in the front courtyard. Out of breath, she entrusted her portmanteau to an enterprising lad atop the coach and mounted the coach steps.

Inside the taproom, Sir Gerald mumbled, "I say old chap is 'sat the mail?"

"I believe so," Archie conceded warily.

"Must have a word with the coachman," he insisted.

Archie began to sweat. It simply wouldn't do for Cox to catch sight of Bella—just as she was about to make good her escape. But how to prevent such a catastrophe?

Suddenly, Sir Gerald sprang to his feet. With sinking heart, Archie realized his only option was to plant him a facer. Doubling his fists Archie skirted the table. But, to his utter astonishment, before he came within arm's reach, Sir Gerald's eyes glazed and his wafer-thin frame dropped over like a dead stick.

Archie winced as Sir Gerald's head hit the table top with a dull thud. However, after mulling things over, Archie gave a nonchalant shrug. At best, Cox would wake with a hangover; at worse, a sore noggin.

Archie rushed from the taproom toward the front entrance of the Rose and Crown. He arrived barely in time to see the Royal Express pull away with Bella seated next to the window. A wide grin split his face. As far as Sir Gerald was concerned, Bella would vanish without a trace.

However, as Archie watched the coach grow smaller and smaller, his mood became introspective. Although friends once more, he faced an uphill battle convincing Bella he was a reformed character. She had no idea, of course, that the innovative methods he had instituted since his father had appointed him bailiff had proved so successful that for the first time in memory the estate was turning a profit. But he was not about to tell her. Granted he had faults; he was no braggard!

Archie frowned. What a pity he had not realized he loved the taking minx until after she had refused his offer. He had been tempted to tell her about the bargain he had struck with his godfather. He had done nothing of the kind, of course. He would sooner cut off his arm than break his word to the crusty old nobleman.

Nonetheless, Archie was not about to give up his goal. Despite Bella's obstinacy, he meant to wed her. Indeed, the instant he was free from prior obligations, he intended to join her in London. It only made sense. With her in town, he could ill afford to dawdle in the country.

Four

Lady Ponsonby sat up quite suddenly in bed, hazel eyes turbulent. Her soft, slender hands clutched a corner of a peach-hued satin bed quilt as though she envisioned being cast adrift into a cold, inky sea, where if she were to let go she would most certainly drown.

Disoriented, groggy from sleep, Hermione gazed about in the dimness, drinking in clues as to her whereabouts. She took in a thin ribbon of sunlight peeping through a slight split in heavy, nut-brown window hangings.

Her green-brown eyes darted to the bedside stand where a Meissen cup and saucer rested, a curl of steam rising from the cup's contents. The sharp taste of fear melted away as she recognized the boudoir's luxurious appointments and pleasing color scheme of peach and ecru accented with a rich nut-brown.

A tiny frown made inroads in her forehead. Obviously, Daisy, the new chambermaid, had awakened her. She would have a thing or two to say to Mrs. Harris about this! That the housekeeper had permitted the green, country lass to deliver her morning chocolate put Lady Ponsonby in a temper. Daisy might do nicely as a scullery maid doing menial tasks under Cook's eye, and perhaps might, in time, become an unexceptional housemaid. But that was all far in the future. At present, the girl was too clumsy to be allowed inside her ladyship's boudoir.

Besides why hadn't Elsbeth fetched her morning chocolate? *Because she's annoyed with me,* Hermione admitted ruefully. *And with good reason!*

A delicate flush highlighted my lady's cheekbones as she recalled her most recent fall from grace. Yesterday morning, Hermione and her personal maid had gone by carriage to Bond Street to purchase satin ribbons and lace to trim an afternoon gown and. . . . Hot needles of guilt prickled along the surface of Hermione's flawless skin. Elsbeth had been disgusted with her mistress's lack of restraint.

Her ladyship's thoughts took a selfish turn. With the passage of years, she thought that Elsbeth would have learned to take her mistress's lapses in stride. After all, Elsbeth had been her abigail ever since Hermione had made her come-out before London Society. Furthermore, since dear Robert's death, her abigail was one of the few people who knew her ladyship's secret. At times, Elsbeth's pious sermonizing cut to the quick and her ladyship entertained the idea of pensioning her off and acquiring a new personal maid who would be ignorant of her mistress's shortcomings.

But for how long would the new abigail remain in the dark? Hermione sighed. No, ridding herself of her present maid would be a grave mistake. At least Elsbeth was genuinely fond of her. Besides, while in private she did not hesitate to ring a peal over her ladyship's head whenever her mistress tumbled from grace, Elsbeth became a veritable tigress on those rare occasions when her ladyship's reputation fell under a cloud of suspicion.

A light scratching on the bed chamber door put an end to Hermione's introspection. "Come in."

Mrs. Harris entered. Bustling about, the housekeeper opened the velvet drapes and clucked disapprovingly at the untouched cup of chocolate, now tepid. Her ladyship, finding Mrs. Harris's officious manner something of a trial before breakfast, just managed to check a frown.

"My lady, there's a young person in the hall who claims to be your niece. Do you wish me to get rid of the encroaching pretender."

Lady Ponsonby took the housekeeper's smug skepticism with a grain of salt. Obviously, the young lady downstairs had not impressed her favorably but, as Harris had hired Daisy, her ladyship did not consider the woman's judgment infallible.

Besides, although Hermione had neglected to inform the servants, she was expecting her niece— though by no means so soon. Why she had barely posted the letter inviting Isabella up to London. How could the girl have arrived in town already?

Hermione's expression reflected her agitation. She needed more time to adjust to the awesome responsibility of taking an orphan under her wing. If only her dear husband were still at her side to act as buffer as he had in the past. Tears pricked behind her eyes. Dearest, Robert, how she missed him!

"Shall I send the shameless baggage off with a flea in her ear?" Mrs. Harris inquired.

"No such thing!" her ladyship cried. "Tell Symonds to make my niece comfortable in the blue drawing room while I dress."

Harris paled. "Your niece, my lady?"

"Indeed. And send Elsbeth to me at once."

"I doubt she's on the premises. I saw her slip out the side door earlier."

"Fustian!" *Elsbeth would fly into a pet today of all days!* Hermione struggled to get a grip on to her temper. "In that case, send me Millie instead."

"It's Millie's day off. What about Daisy?"

"Daisy! I'd rather dress myself. That troublesome goosecap woke me from a sound sleep. I'll thank you to keep her out of my way until she's better trained. Tell Symonds I'll ring when I'm ready to receive."

"Very well, your ladyship." The housekeeper started to withdraw.

"Stay a minute, Harris. I almost forgot. In future, kindly oblige me by referring to my niece in a more civil manner, if you please."

Mrs. Harris's ruddy complexion deepened to a beet red. "I am sorry to have given offense my lady. However I was told nothing of her expected arrival."

"Perfectly true," her ladyship admitted, softening her tone. "I didn't look for Isabella quite so soon. However since she is now under my roof, I want her to feel welcome."

"Indeed, my lady, I assure you, I shall take pains to make her comfortable."

"I'm confident you will, Harris. Now do run along and get things marching."

After Mrs. Harris departed, Lady Ponsonby seated herself at her dressing table. Picking up her silver-backed brush, she began to pull it through her hair. Whatever had possessed her to invite the girl? Why, she was no more suited to serve as a model of correct conduct to her niece than the girl's father! One thing you could say for Reggie, he's never been a hypocrite. Hermione's brother had never made any bones about his shortcomings, whereas she was forever obliged to cover her tracks and live in daily fear that the darker side of her nature would come to light. What would Isabella think of her if that should happen?

Lady Ponsonby would be the first to admit she was not the ideal person to be in charge of a young innocent. Her head spun as she contemplated the harm she might cause. Yet what was the alternative? She could hardly turn her niece out into the street.

A fresh wave of guilt assailed her. She should have written Isabella immediately after she had received her letter informing her of Reggie's death. The poor child must have been desperate by the time Hermione finally responded.

If only, she reasoned, she had been blessed with children of her own, she'd have a better idea of how to go on. A look of pain crossed her countenance. Early in her marriage—when she still hoped to produce an heir—she had managed to control her deplorable tendency. But once she found she could never bear a healthy child, she could no longer fend off the troublesome flaw in her character.

Robert, bless his heart, had elected to stand by her. She had loved her husband deeply and would be forever grateful to him for shielding her from social disgrace.

Hermione straightened her shoulders. Somehow or other, she must conquer the odious habit for Isabella's sake. She would never forgive herself if she were responsible for embroiling her innocent niece in a scandal.

A half hour passed before my lady had completed her toilet and summoned the courage to face Isabella. Before she lost her nerve, she pulled the servant's bellcord.

To Isabella, the wait seemed interminable. Glancing about, she felt awed by the drawing room's sumptuous appointments. She admired the Axminster carpet and the ormolu clock resting on the mantelpiece of the Adam fireplace. With the soft pads of her fingers, her hand skimmed the satinwood inlay top of a Sheraton knee-hole desk. She tried to envision her aunt seated there writing letters, but failed abysmally. Which was only to be expected, Isabella conceded, considering she had never laid eyes on her aunt before.

More to the point, having always been as poor as a church mouse, it was a little daunting to contemplate living, even briefly, with a noblewoman who appeared to be as rich as King Midas.

A faint smile nudged the corners of her mouth. Whatever would Archie say, if he could see her surrounded by such elegance? Perhaps she had been wrong to turn down his offer, Isabella mused. At least if she had thrown in her lot with him, they would have their mutual penury in common. "Her ladyship is ready to receive you," a footman announced from the threshold. "Follow me, miss."

Climbing the curved staircase, her fingertips drew comfort from the coolness of the teakwood banister. However, as she reached the landing, she experienced a twinge of fear. What if she and Aunt Hermione didn't get on? Her heartbeat accelerated as she observed the footman scratch lightly upon the closed door.

"Come in."

The servant opened the door and stepped inside, motioning Isabella to follow. "My lady, your niece, Miss Isabella Cox," he intoned.

Dazzled, Isabella caught her breath. Can this hazel-eyed beauty really be my aunt? she wondered with a surge of familial pride.

She stole another glance. In repose, a faint suggestion of melancholy touched her aunt's face. Then, a wisp of a smile enlivened her ladyship's classical features as she rose gracefully to welcome her niece with outspread arms.

"My dear, you are the picture of your mother."

"Am I?" Isabella's sapphire-blue eyes mirrored surprise. "There is no likeness of her at Cox Manor and I've often wondered. Did you know her well?"

"Indeed, Lucinda and I were bosom bows." Lady Ponsonby tucked one of Isabella's wayward curls back into line. "Blond like your mama's. Reggie worshiped your mother's hair."

"Did she meet my father through you, Aunt?"

"I fear so." Lady Ponsonby looked rueful.

Isabella laughed. "From your tone, I gather my father was ever the reprobate."

Her aunt awarded her a look of gentle reproof. "Reggie never got over her death."

"I suspected as much. He never liked me above half, you know. I gather because I'm a female instead of the son he wanted."

Her ladyship's features mirrored indignation. "How beastly of Reggie to take his disappointment out on you!"

"I fear I've painted him a monster. Father wasn't cruel to me, merely indifferent." Isabella decided to steer the conversation into a less volatile channel. "I trust my unannounced arrival is not too inconvenient?"

"Not in the least. I'm happy that you came to me so promptly, though I will own I didn't expect to see you quite this soon."

"It wouldn't have done to stay on once the new owner appeared at Cox Manor," said Isabella.

"I suppose not."

"Rest assured I only intend to impose upon your hospitality until I can secure a post as a lady's companion."

Her ladyship made no effort to hide her astonishment. "Lady's companion? My dear, Isabella, you must be joking. I cannot allow it! Besides, there's no need. Robert left me quite plump in the pocket. Pray don't speak of such a foolish notion again."

"I appreciate your kindness, Aunt, but I don't wish to be beholden. I feel I should make my own way."

Hermione looked vexed. "Isabella, I positively forbid it. As a lady of quality, I expect you to behave with suitable decorum. Do I make myself clear?"

"But Aunt—"

"Isabella, I refuse to discuss this further."

"Yes, ma'am." Not wishing to distress her aunt, she subsided with uncharacteristic meekness.

"There's a good girl! Let's have a look at you. Turn around slowly."

When Isabella came full circle, Lady Ponsonby bade her be seated.

"Your posture is good, however, if the gown you're wearing is a sample of the state of your wardrobe, tomorrow we must hie to Bond Street to see you properly outfitted."

"A new wardrobe? I cannot afford it."

Lady Ponsonby arched an eyebrow. "I can."

"I couldn't let you do that," said Isabella.

"My dear, I must beg you not to oppose me at every turn. Pray tell me why you cannot? You look a quiz in that shabby dress. Not only is it out of style, its seams are about to burst. Not to mention, the sleeves don't quite reach your wrists."

Stung by her aunt's acid appraisal, Isabella said tartly, "I hardly think several hours inside a rackety mail coach has improved my appearance one whit. I know my gown doesn't fit me. How could it? I've grown two inches since it was made up for me three years past?"

Her ladyship's countenance drained of color as she staggered a few steps backward. "Mercy! Do you mean to say you came all the way to London in a public coach?"

A pleading expression came into Isabella's eyes. "I had to, Aunt Hermione. Father didn't leave me a farthing. Ned, our groom, lent me his savings. It barely covered my meals once I'd purchased my ticket."

"Don't fret, child. I'm not vexed with you, but with myself. Can you ever forgive your rattle-brained aunt? When you mentioned straitened circumstances in your letter, I never dreamed you meant you had no private mode of transportation at your disposal. Or even an abigail to bear you company."

"Abigail? Do you seriously imagine Father would pay out funds he might wager to hire a personal maid for me?"

"How dull-witted of me! I'd quite forgotten what a nip-cheese Reggie was, apart from his own pleasures. You came alone then?"

Isabella nodded. "I can only be grateful your invitation arrived when it did. You see, the new heir would not be discouraged by my refusal to wed him. He made my life a misery by dogging my every step for the sennight I passed under *his* roof. Even my chaperone's frown of disapproval at his over-solicitous behavior failed to make an impression. I confess his persistence put me into a rare fidget."

Amusement danced in Hermione's hazel eyes. "How trying for you. I gather Reggie's heir is something of a slowtop?"

"He doesn't lack brains, but understanding! I vow he had no inkling his prosery set my teeth on edge. Furthermore, his idea of proper female deportment is positively gothic!" Isabella stated feelingly. "I daresay it is unkind of me to say so, though."

"For my part, I think it very kind of you to drop me a hint. Should I ever be so unfortunate as to meet this paragon, thanks to you, I'll be able to nip his prosery in the bud before I'm reduced to nodding off in public."

"You are joking. Too bad of you, Aunt!" Isabella teased, then afraid she'd offended, said hastily, "I beg your pardon."

"Not at all, dearest. I quite deserved a setdown. Never stand on ceremony with me, child!" Her ladyship's countenance sobered. "It's a miracle you managed to arrive on my doorstep unharmed. Since you have, I won't tease you further on that head. As to the question of new clothes, do give over. I am devastated when I realize you haven't had a new gown in three years. Robert's death oppressed my spirits. In my grief, I've neglected you shamefully. My conscience will give me no peace unless you will allow me to make amends by refurbishing your wardrobe."

"Pray don't distress yourself, Aunt Hermione. If it will make you happy, truly I should enjoy a few new gowns."

"And so you should! Furthermore, I shall insist upon giving you regular pin money and beg you not to be so ragmannered as to object!"

"No, indeed," Isabella said soothingly.

"Very sensible. Now I believe I'll order a breakfast tray brought to us here. I would imagine you're feeling peckish after your arduous journey."

"I must own I'm quite famished, Aunt," said Isabella.

When Mrs. Harris answered her summons, her ladyship ordered a generous tray. "Once we've eaten, be so good as to show my niece to a bedchamber? I declare the poor child looks positively hagged."

A little over an hour later, hunger pangs sated, Isabella climbed into a four-poster bed and closed her eyes. Exceedingly tired, she expected to fall sound asleep in a matter of minutes. Instead, glimpses of her trip up to London in the mail coach kept flitting through her mind.

Lying in bed, drifting in and out of consciousness, she wrinkled her nose as she recalled the pipe smoker, befouling the close, stale air inside the public carriage with a cheap blend of tobacco.

What a contrast to her luxurious surroundings here in Berkeley Square! And what a dear her aunt was! Isabella could scarcely take it all in. Thank goodness she had contrived, despite all the obstacles strewn in her path, to come safely to roost on Lady Ponsonby's doorstep.

Five

"Checkmate," Archie said silkily.

The Earl of Chandos glowered across the game table at his godson and then down at the chessboard. "Spiked my guns have you?"

"So it appears. A final game before you retire?"

His lordship shrugged. "Why not?"

Archie set to work rearranging the chess pieces. Because the bookroom was, as usual, overheated, he had shed his coat and waist-coat and sat playing in his shirtsleeves.

"How is it you're not out hobnobbing with society instead of playing nursemaid?" asked the earl.

Archie looked discomfited. "One needs invitations to hobnob."

"Stuff. Why not pass the evening at White's? Why do you think I sponsored your membership?"

"Obviously so I might rub shoulders with peers of the realm. But as I've given you my word not to gamble, it would be stupid of me to frequent that excellent gentlemen's club evenings."

"I must admit I hadn't thought of the matter in that light," Chandos conceded.

"I do make a point of dropping in there most afternoons. Today, as a matter of fact, I ran across a crony from Oxford. Quite a surprise. When we parted at Newmarket, he said nothing about coming to town."

Archie sucked in his breath. The recollection of the single day at the track still had the power to make his palms sweat. Tempted to gamble, but mindful of his promise to the earl, he'd been miserable. Thus, though proud of himself for not betting on a single race, he was not about to test his willpower by hanging about White's.

"A crony? Splendid! You'll find your feet, lad. It's early days yet."

Archie chuckled good-naturedly. "Stop pitching it rum, sir. You've been on edge ever since I confided Isabella Cox rejected my offer."

"Fustian! If you ask me, you're well rid of the silly ninnyhammer!"

Archie bit his tongue. Bella might be stubborn, but she was not silly. He wondered how she was faring in town. Had Lady Ponsonby found her a post? Or had her ladyship insisted Bella make her bow to society?

His fingers tightened around a pawn. For all he knew, Lady Ponsonby had already lined up a host of eager young bucks anxious to engage Bella's affections. Tight-lipped, he fought down a surge of panic. He ought to have called at Berkeley Square the instant he arrived. Instead, he had put off doing so in the mistaken belief that they would run into each other at some tonnish affair.

But cultivating the cream of society took longer than he had anticipated. The corners of his mouth curved in a self-mocking smile. So much for his scheme to impress Bella with his social address.

"Wipe that silly grin off your face," the earl commanded.

His godfather's exasperated tone jarred Archie from reverie. "Sir?"

Chandos snorted. "Just as I thought. Off in a fog."

"Sorry, sir. You were saying . . . ?"

The old man glared at him. "Depend upon it. You'll cease to pine for Miss Cox, once you meet the current crop of eligible females."

"As to that, sir, Jon promises to use his influence to get me invited to some of the more select social affairs."

"Excellent!"

"It's your move," said Archie, deftly turning the conversation.

"So it is." Chandos studied the chess-board. "This crony of yours . . ." He repositioned his rook but kept his fingers around the piece while contemplating the wisdom of his move. "What's his surname?"

"Lansbury. Jonathan Lansbury."

"Hmm. Does he, by chance, hail from Devon?"

"As a matter of fact he does."

Chandos thought a moment. "Well-connected family, the Lansburys. I'd like to meet the young cub the next time he calls."

"As you wish. Have you completed your turn or do you wish to cogitate further?"

When his godfather neither answered nor loosened his grip on the chess piece, Archie shot him a questioning glance— only to discover the earl regarding him intently.

"Something on your mind, sir?"

"Aye. How often do you see your father these days?"

Archie's chuckle contained a bitter note. "Very seldom. Which is perhaps just as well, since we seldom see eye to eye. When he showed up at Brainridge Hall just after harvest, I tried to get him to plow some of the profits realized from a bumper crop of wheat back into the estate for badly-needed improvements."

The earl's expression was shrewd. "Judging by the glum look on your face, I gather he refused."

"Emphatically. He relishes riding to the

hounds. Never mind that Brainridge Hall has been the principle seat of the family since time immemorial, he determined to squeeze every penny he can glean from it, so he can pour it into the Leicestershire property."

"I daresay keeping the string of hunters in prime condition is devilishly expensive."

"Without a doubt," Archie agreed dryly. "As a baliff, I find it so frustrating. I flatter myself that I've an affinity for farming, but it's impossible to institute needed changes without funds and father refuses to listen to reason."

"So what shall you do? Throw in the towel?"

"Never!"

"But your hands are tied, are they not?"

"Not precisely." Archie gave a tortured sigh. "Once again I shall tighten my belt and use part of my salary as bailiff to underwrite the cost."

"How noble."

A wry expression flitted across Archie's broad, affable features. "Gammon. Stupid more like. But I can't help it. Truth to tell, I'm as mad about farming as my father is about fox hunting. But that's enough discussion about me. We've a game in progress."

"Quite," the earl agreed. "It's your move."

Little was said for the next three-quarters of an hour as both players concentrated upon the chessboard. But finally the companionable lull in the conversation was shattered by Archie's cry.

"Checkmate!"

The earl studied the board, then sighed. "I concede. My game's sadly off. Shall we call it a night?"

"Fine with me. I have to be up at the crack of dawn. Jon's taking me round to Gentleman Jim's Boxing Salon."

"Confound it!" Jonathan Lansbury exclaimed as he regarded two magnificent specimens of manhood stripped to their waists and stalking each other in the raised roped-off area of the fashionable gymnasium. "I was so dashed certain all we need do was to get here earlier than usual to have a go with Gentleman Jim, but that curst Irishman's before us."

Archie eyed the pugilists for several seconds before he said, "Grandison seems able to hold his own."

"Think so? Keep your eyes peeled. Gentleman Jim's got the handiest pair of fives in boxing."

But Archie scarcely glanced at the ex-champion. Eager to have a word with the shrewd Irish horse trader, he edged closer to the ring.

Suddenly, Gentleman Jim scored a hit.

Malcolm Grandison crumbled to the floor. Archie winced.

"What a facer!" Jon crowed. "Jackson's punch flashed like lightning. I'll lay odds Grandison never saw it coming."

"I daresay, he didn't, else he'd have ducked," said Archie.

Gentleman Jim apologized for the unintentional hit. Grandison begged him not to fuss, but Jackson paid no heed. Instead, he beckoned to an urchin hovering at ringside. The lad scrambled between the ropes and handed the downed pugilist a turkish towel.

Rising, Grandison wiped perspiration off his face, then draped the towel round his neck and made for the ropes. Eager to serve, the urchin bounded forward to spread the thick strands of braided hemp wide enough apart to allow him to make a graceful exit.

Outside the ring, he spotted Archie and somehow managed a feeble grin. "Top of the morning to you, boyo."

"How's your jaw, sir?"

"Painful. However, it will mend."

"Good. You recall my friend, Jon?"

"Certainly. What brings you here so early?"

Archie chuckled. "Jon's dying to go a few rounds with Gentleman Jim. He's even willing to forgo sleep to achieve his goal."

The Irishman's eyes brimmed with irony. "My mishap appears to be your opportunity.

Seize your chance, Lansbury. Climb into the ring."

"Capital suggestion," said Jon, already in motion.

The instant Jon had moved out of earshot, Grandison addressed Archie, "Called on your young lady yet?"

"No, sir," Archie mumbled, averting his gaze.

Grandison cocked an eyebrow. "Faint heart never won fair maiden."

"True. I intend to call on her soon."

"That's the spirit, boyo!" He gave Archie a hearty slap on the back before he walked on.

However, striding toward his dressing room, Grandison decided that Jackson's blow to his jaw must have addled his wits. He was a fine one to talk. Instead of calling on Hermione, he had procrastinated. But now he would tolerate no more backsliding. It was time he confronted the lovely woman who haunted his dreams.

The jam of fashionable carriages that greeted the Ponsonby coach the instant it turned into Drury Lane made Hermione fretful. "Gracious, what a horrible squeeze! I trust we won't be too late to catch the first curtain."

Isabella peered out the window at the glut of carriages in the narrow street. She doubted they would arrive in time. A pity since, like a child anticipating a peppermint stick, her aunt looked forward to tonight's performance of *The Marriage of Figaro*.

"Well, I for one don't propose to miss a minute of the opening score!" Hermione rapped sharply upon the interior of the carriage roof with her fan.

The coachboy scurried down from his perch. "Wot's amiss, your ladyship?"

"Find us a couple of chairmen to convey us to the entrance. There's a good lad."

Thanks to Lady Ponsonby's ingenuity, she and her niece were ushered into a private box a scant thirty minutes later, when the musicians were still warming up. Settling into a plush velvet chair, Isabella had no time to admire the glittering chandeliers suspended from the theater's vaulted ceiling before the conductor dipped his baton, signaling the musicians to begin.

As the gaslights slowly dimmed, the look of rapt expectancy upon her aunt's lovely face filled Isabella with awe. Part of her astonishment stemmed from the fact that, during the sennight she had spent under her aunt's roof, that lady had seemed quite content to spend most evenings quietly at home. There, to her niece's delight, she often filled the interval between their evening meal and the tea tray by playing the pianoforte.

Isabella's puzzlement vanished. Why of

course! Mozart was the lure that had coaxed her aunt from her hearth this evening. No longer perplexed, Isabella allowed herself to become caught up in the music.

When intermission brought a temporary break in the performance, her ladyship trained her dreamy gaze upon her niece. "Are you enjoying the music, dearest?"

Smiling, Isabella said, "How could I not?"

Behind them, a curtain parted and a well-set-up gentleman in his early forties stepped into their box. Wingshaped ebony eyebrows lent a hint of devilment to his swarthily handsome features. His thick, black hair carried a liberal sprinkling of gray. However, it was his Vandyke beard tipped with silver that lent an air of distinction to his countenance.

Assuming him to be one of her aunt's admirers, Isabella looked askance just in time to see the color drain from Hermione's face.

"Good evening, my lady," he said, bowing over her ladyship's trembling hand. "Would you care to promenade in the lobby?"

He planted a kiss in the palm before he released it. Hermione gasped and, paler than ever, followed the descent of her hand to her lap before glancing up at her tormentor.

"No, thank you, sir," she said, her voice a thready whisper, her hazel eyes glittering with resentment at the liberties he had taken.

"Coward!" His deep baritone chided. "The least you could do is to graciously accede, considering I've followed you all the way from Ireland."

"No one asked you to," she snapped.

"True. But as you left in such haste, I was worried."

"Humbug!"

"By the saints, madam, you try my patience!" The man started to withdraw, but, catching sight of Isabella, looked chagrined. "My lady, in our zeal to cross swords, we've neglected your guest. Who is this beguiling child?"

"Heaven forbid we neglect the social amenities," Hermione mocked. "My niece, Miss Isabella Cox. Bella, this . . . gentleman is Malcolm Grandison, friend and business partner of my late husband."

"Yours, too, my lady, did you permit it," he said with gruff conviction.

As Isabella rose and curtsied, her thoughts were busy. Her aunt seemed attracted to Mr. Grandison, yet skittish. Though Isabella sensed he truly cared for Aunt Hermione, it was obvious she did not trust him.

Which was a pity. Still Isabella did not think his campaign to engage her aunt's affections was entirely hopeless. However, she felt he would stand a better chance if he did not scowl. It unnerved her aunt. Besides, he was better looking when he smiled.

Once again, the curtain parted to admit a

visitor. Isabella's eyes rounded with surprise. "Archie! Whatever are you doing here?"

He laughed. "Spotted you from the pit. Came to pay my respects."

"I don't mean what are you doing in our box. What are you doing in London?"

"Godfather invited me. He wishes me to take in the season."

"You're roasting me."

"No, I ain't. It's the gospel truth." Archie shifted his gaze to Grandison. "Evening, sir."

The Irishman gave a wry chuckle. "Finally got your nerve up, I see. Me too, boyo, me too."

Lady Ponsonby pointedly cleared her throat. Isabella glanced at her, pleased to see her aunt's complexion was again rosy.

Hermione returned her smile. "Dearest, introduce me to your friend."

Isabella could have kicked herself. Her aunt had drilled society manners into her ever since she had arrived. Yet, she'd failed the first test. Cheeks tinged a delicate pink, she hastened to do the honors.

To her astonishment, Archie made her aunt an elegant bow. "Delighted to meet you, ma'am."

"And I you, sir. As the Brainridge property marches in line with Cox land, I assume your acquaintance with my niece is of long-standing."

"Indeed, my lady, I've known Bella since

we were both grubby brats. Do I have your permission to call?"

"Rest assured my niece and I will be delighted to receive you."

"Would either of you ladies care for a glass of lemonade during the next interval?" Grandison inquired.

"Sounds lovely," said Isabella.

"Yes, it does," her aunt agreed, in a voice totally devoid of animation.

Isabella's brow wrinkled. It troubled her that Mr. Grandison's presence seemed to cast a pall upon her aunt's normally ebullient spirits. Nor did she fail to note her ladyship's relief when the warning bell, signaling the imminent rise of the second act curtain, encouraged both gentlemen to take a hasty leave.

The following morning found Isabella in the drawing room, thumbing through the latest copy of *La Belle Assemblee* while her aunt caught up on her correspondence. Symonds entered. "Your ladyship, Mr. Archibald Brainridge desires a private audience with your niece to discuss a personal matter."

Hazel eyes pensive, Hermione regarded her young charge. "Do you wish to receive him alone, dearest?"

"No! That is, I don't if he's come for the purpose I suspect."

"Purpose? Kindly enlighten me."

Isabella blushed. "He made me an offer just before I left for London."

"I see." Hermione regarded her niece thoughtfully. "You refused him, I collect?"

Isabella nodded. "It was the only sensible course. Bad enough he's a fourth son with no prospects, he's a gamester to boot."

"And you think he intends to renew his suit?"

"Of a certainty! Why request a word in private otherwise?"

"My poor child. Tenacity in a suitor you've taken in dislike can be tedious, can it not?"

"Oh, but I don't dislike Archie. It's his gambling I cannot abide." Isabella willed her hands to remain quiet in her lap despite a violent urge to wring them. "To be fair, he claims he's given it up for good, but I beg leave to doubt it."

Hermione rolled her eyes ceilingward. "Dearest, you are much too young to play the cynic. What harm can it do to grant him a few minutes in private?"

"You think I should?"

"Yes, I do." Her ladyship smiled reassuringly. "My dear, don't look so worried. I promise to remain within shouting distance."

"Very well then, I'll see him."

When Archie sauntered into the drawing room, Isabella could not help but admire the excellent cut of his coat of superfine wool.

Her gaze riveted upon his broad shoulders and his strong, husky frame. Her pulses raced as he bowed over her hand. Morever, when he brushed her fingertips with his lips, a swift, charged current shot through her.

Unnerved by her reaction to his merest touch, Isabella sent her aunt a pleading look, which my lady either did not see or chose to ignore.

Rising, Hermione addressed Archie. "Young man, I shall allow you exactly ten minutes alone with my niece."

Archie beamed. "Thank you, my lady."

Her aunt had barely exited before Isabella, who by now was bursting with impatience, wagged a finger at Archie and warned, "If you mean to make me another offer, save your breath."

"No need to fly up into the boughs, Bella," he advised blandly. "My reason for calling is not of a romantic nature."

Perversely annoyed with herself for feeling so crushed because he didn't intend to renew his suit, Isabella asked, "Then why insist upon seeing me alone?"

"Because it's a personal matter. Ned charged me to deliver the proceeds from the sale of your father's mare. Here you are."

He handed her a sack of coins so heavy, she was obliged to use both hands to transfer it to a nearby table.

"How good of you to bring this in person. Do forgive me for playing the shrew."

He gave a negligent wave of his hand. "It is already forgotten."

Bemused, she regarded the sack of coins, "So much for one horse?"

"Stands to reason. Starlight *was* a thoroughbred."

"Very true." Tears stung behind her eyes. "I hope her new owners appreciate her."

"They will if they don't want for sense." He offered her a clean handkerchief.

Isabella bristled. "Put that away. I've no intention of playing the watering pot."

"Course you don't. You've too much bottom."

He stuffed the handkerchief back into a pocket. "Quite a surprise seeing you last night in Drury Lane."

"My aunt adores Mozart."

"Nonetheless, the opera's the last place I'd have thought to seek you. Am I to gather you've given up your plan to become a lady's companion?"

"Yes. Aunt Hermione forbids it. Indeed, she insists on standing the nonsense for my first-season."

A hint of sad resignation flickered in Isabella's dark blue eyes. "I only agreed to a season to please her. Nothing will come of it. No one will offer for me as I've no dowry."

"Rubbish!"

"Scoff if you wish. I'm only being realistic."

"Fond of her ladyship I take it?"

"As far as I'm concerned she's top of the trees."

Archie nodded. "How come you ain't in mourning?"

Isabella's steady gaze faltered. "Aunt Hermione has only recently put off the blacks she donned at the death of her husband. She insists the very thought of me in black crepe is enough to sink her spirits."

"Make's sense," Archie admitted. The expression in his gray eyes softened. "You know, my dear, I'd make you another offer in a trice if I thought you'd accept."

"Pray do not. How many times must I state, I won't marry you?"

"Look here, Bella, all I want is a chance to prove I'm trustworthy. Is that too much to ask?"

"Do you take me for a fool? Father was forever swearing off gambling. I lost count of how many mornings he woke with pockets to let. Each time he vowed to quit. But by evening he was always eager to once again approach the gaming tables." Isabella had difficulty choking back tears. "If you want the truth I'm afraid to trust you. I couldn't stand it, should you disappoint me."

"Dash it all, Bella, I ain't a curst loose

screw like your father. If I give you my word I won't gamble, you can bank on it."

A wistful look in her eyes, Isabella whispered, "I'd like to believe you, truly I would, but I cannot."

"If that don't beat all! All these years I thought you were pluck to the backbone and now I discover you've got about as much rumgumption as a garden worm," Archie raved. "At least I'm willing to admit I've a few habits that need mending. But not you, Bella. I'm willing to lay odds, you think your character can't stand any improvement."

Then, without giving Isabella a chance at rebuttal, Archie stormed out of the drawing room in high dudgeon.

Six

"Walking? Never say you ventured out alone!" Seated at her dressing table, Lady Ponsonby returned the Meissen china cup to its saucer with a forceful clunk.

"No such thing, ma'am. I took Daisy," Isabella answered.

"Merciful heavens!" Her ladyship looked horrified. "When I think of you racketing about the streets with goodness only knows what riff-raff, it quite puts me in a taking! Whatever made you take Daisy? No doubt she was too busy gawking at the sights and tripping over her own feet to be of the least use. Why didn't you ask Millie to accompany you? She'd have steered you away from the seamier streets in favor of those frequented by the *ton.*"

"Because I prefer Daisy. Anyway, we merely went for a short stroll. I assure you we met no one exceptional," Isabella said soothingly.

"Well there's no accounting for tastes, I suppose," Hermione said more calmly.

Lady Ponsonby's dresser gave her mistress's coiffure a final pat and asked, "Will this do, your ladyship?"

Isabella watched as Hermione gazed into the gilt-framed mirror above her dressing table. The abigail had arranged her ladyship's thick brown hair, parted in the center and twisted into a soft chignon that hugged the nape of her neck.

"Very nice, Elsbeth. Now be so good as to fetch my breakfast tray? Toast and jam will do, as I wish to allow plenty of time for our excursion to Bond Street."

"Mayhap I should ring for Millie," Elsbeth suggested. "While she sees to your tray, I can be laying out the clothes you wish to wear."

"No, I want you to fetch it. It will give me a chance to have a private coze with my niece."

Her ladyship met the abigail's rebellious gaze with unwavering aplomb. The battle of wills ended with Elsbeth's capitulation. However, the resentful glare she tossed her mistress's niece before quitting the room left Isabella shaken. Bewildered as well, for she could think of nothing she'd done to earn the abigail's animosity.

Self-consciously, Isabella smoothed the skirt of her walking ensemble. The cerulean blue overdress was made of heavy twill fabric and had a profusion of tiny buttons running down the fitted bodice to her waist. From that point on, the outer garment fell open to the floor, revealing an underdress of striped blue-and-white chintz.

Lady Ponsonby's face broke into a smile. "Dearest, it gratifies me immensely to see you rigged out in something modish. I must confess blue vastly becomes you."

"Thank you. It proved an ideal choice for my walk as the air's rather brisk this morning."

"Ah yes, your walk with Daisy. What you see in that awkward creature amazes me."

"She's as overwhelmed by London as I am. I daresay once she feels comfortable, her clumsiness will vanish."

A glimmer of mischief danced in Lady Ponsonby's eyes. "Indeed, you seem quite taken with the girl. Care to give her a trial as your abigail?"

Eyes shining, blissfully unaware she was being teased, Isabella gave her aunt an affectionate hug. "I should like it above all things!"

Her ladyship laughed. "Off with you, infant, so I may ready myself for today's shopping excursion."

"Another one, Aunt? My wardrobe is bursting."

"Nonetheless, while you've enough frocks suitable for morning and afternoon wear, you've next to nothing for evening."

"My rose silk is lovely."

"True, but I must beg your indulgence, Isabella. I should soon weary of seeing you at the dinner table in the same gown night after night, however charmingly it becomes you. Furthermore, you've already worn it to Drury Lane. Since you know my passion for the Italian opera, I must insist you acquire enough gowns to be fashionably attired whenever you accompany me there."

Isabella's voice held a trace of exasperation as she said, "I might as well give over. It's a waste of breath to argue with you, Aunt."

Lady Ponsonby chuckled softly. "I am glad you've decided to be sensible. Can you be ready to leave in an hour?"

"Certainly. Now do excuse me. I'm famished."

In the breakfast room, Isabella helped herself to a generous helping of scrambled eggs and several triangular pieces of toast from the sideboard. Her brisk morning walk had sharpened her appetite. Besides, judging from past shopping trips, there was little likelihood she'd get anything further to eat until their return to Berkeley Square late in the afternoon.

Her appetite temporarily sated, Isabella retreated to her bedchamber to pace the carpet, her conscience vaguely uneasy. What was the matter with her anyway? Moldering away at Cox Manor, she had often yearned for stylish new gowns. So why did her aunt's generosity bother her so much?

Isabella's introspective mood was shattered by her aunt's entrance. Her ladyship's musical laughter echoed throughout her niece's charmingly-furnished bedchamber.

"Your door was ajar so I let myself in. Such a long face, dearest. It is very bad of you to cast me in the role of an ogress merely because I refuse to take you about shabbily dressed. Do humor me. I can well afford to indulge myself. I'm quite selfish, you see, and refurbish your wardrobe simply because it pleasures me."

Isabella laughed a trifle shakily. "I'm an ungrateful wretch."

"No such thing. Your scruples do you credit so long as you don't become a dead bore. I've been so lonely since Robert died, and find having you living under my roof quite diverting."

Her aunt's eyes glistened with unshed tears. "Tie on your bonnet," she ordered, adopting a brisker tone. "The carriage is due to draw up to the front door any minute."

Isabella donned a cream straw bonnet, embellished with forget-me-nots circling the crown and tied it under her chin with yellow satin ribbons. She gathered her gloves, reticule and a blue-and-white-striped chintz parasol that matched her underskirt.

Outside the town house, matched bays harnessed to her aunt's barouche awaited them. A footman assisted Isabella to climb into the carriage where she took a seat beside Lady Ponsonby. Isabella was still getting settled when Elsbeth scuttled aboard and assumed a seat facing the rear.

As the coachman guided the fashionable barouche away from Berkeley Square, Isabella frowned. Elsbeth's dogged determination to accompany her mistress on each and every shopping excursion puzzled her— not to mention why her aunt put up with such a bossy servant. Not that it was any business of hers, Isabella admitted, resolutely fixing her gaze on the passing scenery.

The team maintained a steady trot until it turned onto Bond where the flow of traffic forced them to travel at a slower pace. Minutes later, they halted in front of Madame Leone's.

As the coachman pulled away from the curb, Lady Ponsonby handed Elsbeth a list of commissions to undertake while she and her niece consulted the dressmaker. Elsbeth's sour mien hinted at a case of acute dyspepsia as she set off.

A bit later, inside the fashionable establishment, Isabella was coaxed into a white muslin sprigged with dark green that required a final fitting, a chore left to under-seamstresses. As they pinned its hem, she tried not to fidget, wishing they would hurry so she might join her aunt and the dress-maker in their spirited discussion of patterns and delicate fabrics reserved for evening gowns.

Two hours snailed past before she was able to tie on her bonnet again and draw on her white kid gloves. Lady Ponsonby and Madame Leone, with an occasional contribution from Isabella, had decided on a demure white organdy and another gown with white lace bodice and an underdress of pink gauze. After much discussion, an additional gown of the palest yellow muslin was added to make a total of four evening dresses, counting the rose silk hanging in her wardrobe at Berkeley Square. Quite enough, she fervently hoped, as she found standing statue still for fittings quite tedious.

However, no trace of impatience showed on her face as she heard her aunt leave word for Elsbeth to join them at Schomberg House before bidding the dressmaker good afternoon.

Outside Madame Leone's, her aunt said, "Come along, child. There's still accessories to purchase to set off your new gowns."

Lady Ponsonby set a leisurely pace. Isabella cast a wistful look inside the book deal-ers' window as they strolled past. In Pall Mall, they entered Schomberg House, the fashionable emporium operated by Harding and Howell. Her ladyship guided her niece to the shoe section to be fitted with kid evening slippers, one pair tinted pale blue; the other shell pink. Their next stop was a mahogany paneled stall where gloves were purchased to match the slippers.

Assuming they were finally done with shopping, Isabella's spirits rose. Perhaps aunt wouldn't object to a short browse through the book dealers while awaiting their coach's arrival.

"To save time, let's separate," her ladyship suggested. "While you select a fan that takes your fancy, I'll slip over to the ribbon counter to purchase some green braid I need before rejoining you here."

"As you wish, Aunt." Isabella tried not to let her disappointment show at having no time to visit the booksellers.

After a dutiful examination of a variety of fans in the display case, she made a tentative choice of the carved ivory. "If you'll be so good as to set this one aside, I'll fetch my aunt," she informed the shopgirl.

Isabella located the ribbon counter with no trouble but could see no sign of her aunt. Her eyes scanned the enormous room, seeking her ladyship. At last she sighted her standing near the jewelry counter. Isabella rushed impulsively forward, only to check her stride when she noticed Elsbeth was with her. Furthermore, both mistress and servant had assumed the stance of banty hens and were obviously engaged in a heated brangle. Curious to learn what they were quarreling about, Isabella edged cautiously closer.

As she came within earshot, Elsbeth shook an admonishing finger at her mistress and said, "Be sensible, my lady. Your jewelry case is already overflowing. You don't need a diamond pendant."

Just then, a cluster of customers entered from the street creating a draft that caused teardrop crystals suspended from overhead chandeliers to tinkle. Simultaneously, the play of wavering candlelight reflected in cut glass prisms bounced sparkles off the diamond pendant under discussion.

Lady Ponsonby sighed. "No doubt you are right. Yet, it's so lovely, it's hard to resist."

The wistful note in her aunt's voice sparked Isabella's anger. How dare Elsbeth presume to tell Aunt Hermione how to spend her money? Had Elsbeth been her abigail instead of her aunt's, Isabella wouldn't have tolerated such highhanded behavior for a minute.

A stately matron moved into Isabella's line of vision, breaking her concentration. At first, the matron's face registered as a pleasant blank. Then, all of a sudden, a flicker of recognition dawned in her dark eyes.

"Well I never! Hermione Ponsonby. Fancy running into you after all these years."

Hermione gazed sharply at the matron. "Amanda? Is it truly you?"

"Most assuredly. My dear, I vow you're as lovely as ever. But that's to be expected from an Incomparable."

After a warm embrace, the two ladies stepped gracefully apart.

Hermione laughed gayly. "You scarcely look at your last prayers either, my dear." She nudged Isabella forward. "Amanda, I'd like to present my niece, Isabella Cox."

"Reggie and Lucinda's offspring?" The matron's dark eyes peered at Isabella with frank curiosity.

Smiling, Hermione turned to her niece. "My dear, this is Lady Lansbury. She and I and your dear mother all attended the same ladies' seminary ages ago."

"How do you do, ma'am." Isabella dipped a curtsy and then lifted her gaze to study her aunt's friend.

Lady Lansbury looked rueful. "Too bad my daughter isn't with me today. Fanny would so enjoy meeting Isabella. Unfortunately she was feeling a bit hagged this morning and I insisted she rest so she will be fresh tonight. We plan to attend Lady Sefton's rout. Shall we see you there, Hermione?"

Lady Ponsonby gave a nervous laugh.

"Heavens no. I no longer move in such elevated circles."

"I know you've rusticated for many years on your Irish estate, but surely when in London . . ."

Hermione sighed. "I fear I don't socialize in town either. So don't look to see me at any tonnish affairs. I should love to meet your daughter though. I am persuaded Isabella would enjoy her company. Perhaps you would bring Fanny to tea one day soon?"

"I'd be delighted. Give me your direction."

A trill of musical laughter escaped Hermione. "I know it's been ages, Mandy, but surely you remember our house in Berkeley Square."

Amanda Lansbury gave a rueful chuckle. "I confess it quite slipped my mind. Don't forget, I, too, have lived a countrified existence for the past decade and a half. Is Thursday afternoon convenient?"

"Thursday is fine. Now I fear we must go. My coachman will be cross as crabs if we keep the horses standing."

"I, too, must fly. I only popped in to buy Fanny a pair of silk stockings." Lady Lansbury graced them with a warm smile. "Until Thursday then."

As they glided past the jewelry counter, Isabella threw her aunt a sidelong glance. Gracious! Aunt was staring wistfully at the diamond pendant again! For the life of her, Isabella couldn't understand why Aunt Hermione did not ignore her abigail's advice and buy it if she fancied it that much.

With a final sigh of regret, her ladyship transferred her gaze to Isabella. "Don't dawdle, dearest. I don't wish to put the coachman in a fidget."

Once ensconced inside the barouche, Isabella studiously avoided Elsbeth's fulminating stare as she mulled over the quarrel she had witnessed. Arguing in public, particularly with an uppity servant was hardly the thing. On the other hand, perhaps she was refining too much on what appeared to be a minor incident, Isabella reasoned.

Her ladyship awarded her niece a warm smile. "Such a treat to run into dearest Amanda after all these years. I'm sure you and Fanny will get on famously."

"I daresay we shall, Aunt," Isabella replied, resolving not to dwell on the puzzling episode any longer.

Seven

Isabella's bravado fizzled as she stood poised at the threshold of the drawing room. Her knees felt none too steady and she was keenly aware of a paper-thin layer of fine moisture that coated her skin. She was still trying to work up the nerve to enter when her aunt glanced in her direction.

"There you are, dearest," Lady Ponsonby called. "Come make Fanny's acquaintance. She's a year younger and—" Her hazel eyes rounded perceptibly as Isabella neared. "Merciful heavens! Who cut your hair?"

"Daisy. But you mustn't scold her, ma'am. I nagged her until she did."

Clearly agitated, Hermione appealed to her guest. "Dearest, Amanda, only look at what she's done to her beautiful hair."

"There, there, Hermione," Lady Lansbury soothed. "It won't answer to fly into the boughs."

"But her long tresses could have been arranged so becomingly," Hermione lamented.

"Just so." Lady Lansbury studied Isabella's appearance, then playfully rapped her knuckles with her fan. "Naughty puss! You've given your aunt quite a shock. Though I must own I find close-cropped curls become you. What's your opinion, Fanny?"

Fanny, a lively girl with a pert snub nose, smiled mischievously. "Short hair's all the rage. She's lucky it curls naturally. How I wish I'd been born with *her* blond tresses instead of inheriting *your* uninteresting brown, Mama."

Her mother laughed. "Such a setdown! Resign yourself, miss. Time enough to complain when they begin to turn gray at the temples like your mama's."

Isabella locked gazes with her aunt. "The instant I saw this style sketched in *La Belle Assemblee,* I couldn't wait to try it. But I should have consulted you first. Do forgive me, ma'am."

Mollified, Lady Ponsonby managed a shaky laugh. "I daresay if I engage one of the modish hairdressers to shape it, it may answer."

"Aunt Hermione, you're a trump."

"Dearest, such language! Pray use terms more befitting a lady." Her ladyship issued a stern frown. "Kindly oblige me by ringing for tea."

Isabella crossed to the bellcord and gave it a firm pull. As she rejoined the group, Fanny grinned and patted the sofa invitingly.

Returning the conspiratorial smile, Isabella sank down beside her.

Lady Lansbury fixed her gaze upon her hostess. "As I started to explain before we were diverted by your niece's entrance, since Fanny has turned seventeen I've brought her up to London for her come-out."

"Fanny's quite pretty, Amanda," Hermione observed, her expression wistful as her glance touched Isabella briefly. "I am persuaded the young blades will flock about her at all the balls, eager to fill her dance card."

Isabella was amused at the way the tips of Fanny's ears pinkened in response to Aunt Hermione's praise. Yielding to impulse, she gave the girl's hand a squeeze. Fanny flashed an impish grin and rolled her eyes, obliging Isabella to choke back a giggle.

"I pray you are right. Since I've only one daughter, it behooves me to see her properly launched," Lady Lansbury averred. "Though heaven only knows what mischief my three sons are into back in Devon."

"Three sons, Amanda? How fortunate!"

"Four. Jonathan's in town for the season. I'm counting on him to squire us about."

"You must miss the other boys."

"I do. But Lansbury wouldn't hear of them living in town. He's convinced country air is healthier. Actually, I don't worry about the boys overmuch. Their father will see that they toe the line. Lansbury did promise to come to London when the season's in full swing for Fanny's sake, but if I know my husband, first chance he gets, he'll hie back to his precious land."

Lady Ponsonby chuckled. "Rob felt the same attachment to the Irish countryside. He only traveled to town when he had to for business reasons."

"Did you never accompany him, Hermie?"

"Uh . . . no."

Her aunt appeared ill-at-ease. Obviously her friend's question had disturbed her. Isabella turned to Fanny determined to steer the conversation into safer channels. "How marvelous to be attending balls. Do you have lots of beaux?"

Fanny's creamy complexion blushed a delicate pink. "I've yet to attend my first. And Mama has only ordered one ball gown made up so far. At this rate, I'll be adjudged an ape leader before I make my bow."

"I heard that, young lady. Ungrateful wretch! What a clutch-purse you paint your poor Mama!" Her handsome countenance flushed with embarrassment, Lady Lansbury trained pleading eyes upon her long-lost friend. "We've barely been in town a sennight. And while I think I may be acquitted of being a nip-cheese, I'd be the first to admit I do like to get good value. I took Fanny to a modiste on North Audley that I used to frequent during my salad days. As it had changed hands, I only ordered one evening gown. I own it will do, but there's nothing striking about it. And to be obliged to argue with the woman in charge as to what is suitable for a young miss having her first season is so exhausting."

"Indeed, Amanda, you must try Madame Leone on Bond Street," Lady Ponsonby recommended. "She refuses to argue. You either place yourself in her hands or go elsewhere. Fortunately, she has a marvelous sense of what will suit."

"Sounds like an answer to my prayers. Be assured I shall pay her a visit. Did she make up the charming sprig muslin your niece is wearing?"

"She did. But, Amanda, I must tell you that I find Fanny's dress vastly becoming."

"Thank you. I own the village needlewoman is clever."

Aunt Hermione has good taste, Isabella decided as she ran an admiring eye over Fanny's brown gabardine walking dress, trimmed with a generous flounce of India print calico. She had already caught a glimpse of its matching calico parasol propped against the entrance hall table that held a beige straw bonnet with daisies scattered along the brim.

Suddenly, Isabella's head whirled and she found herself swamped with a feeling that always before she'd firmly nipped in the bud—a sharp longing to have a come-out like other young ladies of her social strata.

But such air dreams would never do! she told herself as she ruthlessly plucked out the twinge of envy she'd felt for the young lady seated beside her.

"My friends call me Bella," she said, forcing a smile. "Do you mind if I call you Fanny?"

"Indeed, I'd much prefer it."

Lady Lansbury lightly tapped her friend's wrist with her fan. "La, Hermione, I imagine you are caught up in a flurry of appointments getting your niece suitably gowned for her come-out."

Isabella was disturbed by the bleak, stricken look that sprang to life in her aunt's eyes. Evidently, Lady Lansbury noted it as well for she asked, "My dear, have you taken ill?"

"No indeed," Aunt Hermione was swift to reassure her.

A rattle of china riveted everyone's attention as Symonds entered with the tea tray. When he withdrew, Hermione poured tea and passed around filled teacups. Isabella was pleased to see some of her aunt's color returning.

"It grieves me that I cannot bring my own niece out," Hermione admitted quietly. "Alas, a past indiscretion I cannot bear to discuss precludes my return to society."

Lady Lansbury sobered. "Now that you

mention it, I recall the bare bones of the incident. I declare I could bite my tongue off. My dear, Hermie, what you must think of me prattling on about Fanny's come-out."

"Perfectly natural you should. Do have one of the little cakes. They're Cook's specialty."

Amanda Lansbury took a tiny square of white cake from a plate of assorted confections. "Forgive me for making mice feet of the business, but would you have any objection to my chaperoning Isabella? It would make it possible for her to enjoy the season."

"It's terribly kind of you to offer, but I shouldn't like to impose."

"Pray don't be so nonsensical! Two spirited young misses are scarcely more trouble than one. Do give over."

"I must admit I've toyed with the idea of hiring a suitable chaperone so Isabella could take in the season. What you suggest would be ideal and it would grieve me to refuse your generous offer, but I wonder if I should take such a risk? I don't think I could bear the raking up of the past."

Lady Lansbury reached over to gently pat her friend's hand. "La, Hermie, what a piece of work you're making of an ancient occurrence. Surely you remember how the tattlebaskets work? Eager to pounce on the latest on-dit, but all's forgotten the instant the next juicy tidbit is offered as grist to their gossipmill."

"Do you know, Amanda, I've missed your refreshing candor. Mayhap I am refining too much on the matter."

"Of course you are, dearest. I understand why you wish to remain in seclusion, but surely you and I owe it to Lucinda to fire her daughter off. And truly I don't mind in the least chaperoning Isabella along with Fanny."

A wobbly laugh, redeemed by its lilt, escaped Lady Ponsonby's mouth. "If I get your drift, it would be shabby beyond reason for me to deny Isabella a season."

"Dear Hermie, as needle-witted as ever," her friend announced fondly.

Fanny and Isabella exchanged a speaking glance then burst into a fit of the giggles. Startled, the two matrons eyed their charges with trepidation.

Lady Ponsonby sighed, and when next she spoke her tone of voice was a shade sharper. "Isabella, since both of you have finished your tea, perhaps you'd care to show Fanny the garden."

Rising, Isabella said, "Come, Fanny. I vow we both could use an airing."

Fanny cast a pleading look at her mother, who said, "An excellent notion! Run along, pet. I know you're anxious to become better acquainted."

As they strolled arm in arm from the room, Isabella heard Lady Lansbury say, "Even the highest stickler won't take exception to you chaperoning your niece in your own home. So you shall bear the brunt of the morning calls, Hermie, while I, of course, will take Isabella along to the routs and assemblies that Fanny and I attend. I daresay it will all work out quite nicely."

"You are too kind. And, Amanda, should anyone inquire as to the reason I'm in seclusion, I would appreciate it if you would tell them I still grieve for Robert."

"Famous! Now as to the question . . ."

Isabella's eyes met Fanny's. With a guilty start, she realized they were both eavesdropping and hustled her from the room.

After a cursory inspection of the walled garden, the two young misses retired to a stone bench. Lost in thought, Isabella was only peripherally aware of the sweet scent of honeysuckle and gazed with disinterest at trees just beginning to leaf.

"A peaceful spot," Fanny observed after a lengthy silence.

"To be sure," Isabella agreed.

"Good of your aunt to give you a season, is it not? Mayhap some handsome young gentleman will make you an offer."

Isabella shook her head. "No one will offer. I've no dowry, you see, though I suppose I must go along with the farce to please Aunt Hermione."

"Oh, Bella, how sad."

"Indeed," she concurred glumly.

"Even so, the balls will be fun," Fanny insisted. "Surely you mean to enjoy yourself."

"Of course. It would be very ragmannered of me to fall into a fit of the dismals because Aunt Hermione desires to treat me to a season."

"Speaking of your aunt, I can't imagine what her secret is, can you?"

Isabella eyed her companion warily. "No doubt my aunt was refining too much on something best forgotten."

"You disappoint me. I assumed you'd know what she and Mama were going on about. After all she's *your* aunt."

"Well I don't. Anyway, it's most improper for us to pry into her affairs."

"But, Bella, aren't you curious? If she were my aunt, I'd be dying to learn her secret. It has to be something serious to force her to retire from society. I can't imagine what she did, though, can you?"

"Truly, I've no idea, although I confess as a schoolgirl I imagined all kinds of reasons as to why she lived in seclusion."

"Splendid!" Fanny clapped her hands in delight. "Do you remember any?"

A reluctant grin tugged at the corners of Isabella's mouth. "Yes, you incorrigible brat, I do. I once decided Aunt Hermione had contracted the smallpox, and though she survived, it resulted in ruined looks."

"Really, Bella! Since her complexion is flawless, it's plain as a pikestaff that's not the reason. What else?"

Isabella smiled. "Another time I cast Uncle Robert in the role of a jealous spouse, who in a fit of pique challenged one of her admirers to a duel, the resulting kickup forcing her retreat from London society."

"It could have happened, could it not?"

"It could but it's highly unlikely. Uncle Robert was known to be even-tempered."

"Oh." Fanny's spirits flagged, then she brightened. "Never mind. I've thought of a reason."

"Indeed. Let's hear it then."

Fanny covered an impish grin with her hand. "Suppose her husband caught her *in flagrante delicto!*"

Offended, Isabella glared at Fanny. "How dare you! Of all the birdwitted theories, yours takes the palm!"

Mortification shone from Fanny's eyes. "You're quite right to scold me, Bella. I've no business cutting up your aunt's character behind her back. Do forgive me."

For several charged seconds, Isabella maintained a stony silence but finally relented. "Very well. I forgive you."

"I beg you not to repeat my tactless remark," Fanny pleaded. "Your aunt could only be hurt by it and I vow Mama would sink with embarrassment."

"Don't worry, infant. I won't breathe a word. Especially as my own conduct leaves something to be desired. No doubt, my airing of schoolgirl speculations spurred you on."

"It's generous of you to share the blame. I daresay I may be too fond of gothic novels. I collect you aren't as addicted to reading as I am."

"On the contrary, I love to read. Though lately I've nothing to hand."

Fanny's dark eyes lit up. "We must learn the direction of the nearest lending library."

"A capital notion!"

The balance of their conversation was devoted to an exchange of reading tastes. However, once Fanny and her mother left, Isabella's misgivings returned to plague her.

Fancy that! She had not been air-dreaming when she had imagined there was a definite reason behind Aunt Hermione's withdrawal from society. Isabella did not like to think her aunt had been unfaithful, but if she hadn't been discovered in a compromising situation, what in heaven's name had she done?

Eight

The fashionable barouche, Ponsonby crest emblazoned on the carriage doors, passed through the Hyde Park Corner Gate at the stroke of five.

"Splendid afternoon for a drive, is it not, my love?" Lady Ponsonby inquired.

"To be sure," Isabella agreed with false brightness.

There was a slight lurch as the coachman tugged at the reins. A prudent man in Isabella's estimation, he gradually checked the spirited team until they were circling the drive, dubbed Rotten Row by the *beau monde*. As their coach bowled along at a more leisurely pace, Isabella became conscious of her aunt's troubled scrutiny.

"In the mopes, dearest? Would it help to tell me what's amiss?"

"Nothing's amiss," Isabella insisted, a trifle sharply.

Actually she longed to confide in her aunt, but how could she explain her tangled emo-

tions and mental confusion? Truth to tell,
Archie's angry departure had caught her by
surprise. He was usually so good-natured, so
even-tempered, his uncharacteristic temper
perplexed her.

Isabella hid a tiny yawn behind her swiftly
raised hand. A pox on the man! Ever since
he had stomped out of her aunt's house a
fortnight past, she had had trouble sleeping.
That Archie had not been back was a blow
to her pride. Even more aggravating, she
missed him.

"Are you certain you're feeling all the
thing?"

"Pray don't fuss, ma'am. I'm fine, truly I
am."

"In that case, may I suggest you try for a
little animation?" her ladyship suggested,
her tone slightly acerbic. "Indeed your lack
of enthusiasm threatens to cast a blight on
our outing."

Isabella managed a weak smile. "Chalk up
my long face to a restless night."

"How disagreeable to be sure!" Hermione
commiserated. "But are you certain lack of
sleep is *all* that's troubling you? I thought
you might be pining for Mr. Brainridge."

"What, that scapegrace? Never!"

Hermione looked disappointed. "Then
you don't have a *tendre* for that engaging
young gentleman?"

"No, ma'am," Isabella lied. It troubled her

that— although she'd done her best to suppress it— her affection for Archie was still obvious. "What has cast me into the dismals is lack of sleep."

"In that case, I'm glad I pressed you to accompany me. In my opinion, nothing cures insomnia quicker than fresh air."

"I expect you're right."

The truth was, Isabella silently conceded, she'd felt a trifle downpin ever since her silly quarrel with Archie. She was sorry she hadn't handled the matter with more tact, and wishful of mending the breach, she had looked for him at the various social functions she attended with Fanny and Lady Lansbury, but so far their paths had not crossed. Furthermore, although she and Aunt Hermione entertained a steady trickle of morning callers, Archie was not one of their number. Not that she blamed him. She'd hurt his pride. Blast her shrewish tongue.

Useless to brood, she decided, not wishing to cast a pall on the outing. Indeed, she was in perfect charity with her aunt's desire to take a turn or two around the park during the fashionable hour when a goodly portion of the *ton* were either on the strut or circling in smart-looking carriages.

In Isabella's view, Hermione was much too sensitive in regard to a minor discretion, long since forgotten, and ought to make more of a push to cultivate old acquaintances. More selfishly, Isabella hoped to see Archie. If she did, she intended to screw up the courage to ask him to pay her a call so she might put things right between them.

"La! There's Amanda." Her ladyship waved her arm in an effort to catch her friend's attention. "Mandy, my love, over here."

As the open landaulette drew alongside the barouche, Isabella nodded to Fanny seated beside her mother while Lady Lansbury greeted her friend with undisguised pleasure. "Delighted to see you've worked up the nerve to mix in with society a little, Hermie."

Hermione laughed. "Indeed, I cannot imagine why I've resisted joining the daily promenade. With so many of the demimonde taking the air, I scarcely think my presence will cause a ripple of interest."

"So I endeavored to tell you!" Amanda exclaimed. The fond smile she bestowed upon Hermione lingered as she shifted her gaze to Isabella. "I imagine you are looking forward to accompanying Fanny and me to Almacks this evening, are you not?"

"Just so, ma'am. Though I will own I find the prospect of meeting the patronesses a bit daunting."

"Nonsense. They won't eat you."

"La, Mandy, however did you manage to procure a voucher for Bella?" Hermione asked.

"Sally Jersey was most kind once I explained Isabella's circumstances. As a matter of fact, Hermie, she sent you her compliments."

Hermione quirked an eyebrow. "Wonders never cease."

"Look, Mama! There's Jon," Fanny cried.

"My love, I beg you to lower your voice to a tone more befitting a proper young miss in her first season," Lady Lansbury commanded repressively, before maternal curiosity gained the upper hand. "You saw Jon? Where?"

"Too late, Mama! He passed us whilst you were delivering your scold," Fanny replied. "Whizzed by at a spanking clip in a cunning high-perch phaeton with yellow wheels."

"Jon? Racing in Hyde Park! I thought he had more sense."

"If it's any comfort to you, Jon wasn't driving."

"Oh? Who was, pray tell?"

Fanny shrugged. "I've no idea, though judging by his skill, I venture to say he's a top sawyer."

Facial features assuming the air of a martyr, Lady Lansbury heaved a sigh. "Nothing for it but to stay put until Jon comes round again. I mean to deliver a tongue lashing he won't forget in a hurry."

"Indeed, Mama, you must not. Think how embarrassed he'll be if you ring him a peal in front of his friend."

Engrossed in the byplay between mother and daughter, Isabella had only a vague peripheral awareness of the approaching horseman. However, when he halted his mount beside the barouche, her gaze shifted and she recognized Malcolm Grandison.

"Servant, ladies," he said, managing a creditable bow despite the confines of his saddle.

Curious to catch her aunt's reaction, Isabella looked askance. Neither Grandison nor Lady Ponsonby appeared to note her avid interest, no doubt because their attention was too firmly fixed upon each other. A tiny shiver of anticipation rippled along Isabella's spine as she watched the bearded gentleman take firm possession of her ladyship's gloved hand. Passion glittered in his eyes as they drank their fill of Hermione's beautiful countenance.

Since the air currents between them seem to crackle with magnetic awareness, Isabella could not help but question her aunt's professed aversion to the handsome Irishman, especially as she could see for herself how her ladyship's hazel eyes melted as they basked in the warmth of Malcolm Grandison's compelling gaze.

Though loyalty dictated she take her aunt's part, try as she would, Isabella could find no fault with his address. Not only did he behave like a perfect gentleman, the quality and fit of his attire bespoke a skilled tailor, she conceded as she admired the richness of his satin brocade waistcoat. Furthermore, in her opinion, the handsome gold watch tucked into an upper pocket lent just the right touch of sartorial splendor.

Suddenly, one of her aunt's horses reared. The barouche gave a violent lurch and both doors flew open. Isabella grabbed hold of an embedded leather strap and held on for dear life. She managed to keep her seat but Lady Ponsonby toppled from the coach and might have sustained a nasty fall, but for Grandison's quicksilver reaction. He pulled her into a strong-armed embrace and set her before him on his mount.

"Are you all right, my lady?" he asked the shaken noblewoman once her coachman had managed to subdue the unruly horse.

"Yes, that is . . . I . . . I wish to thank you, sir, for breaking my fall," Hermione stammered.

"My pleasure, ma'am. Indeed, I cannot recall when I've held such a delightful armful."

Hermione apparently noting for the first time her close proximity to his hard masculine body, blushed crimson.

Grandison looked as though he meant to take her to task for behaving so missishly. Instead he pressed his lips into a thin line and said in an equable tone of voice, "Once

I'd caught you, I had no choice but to hold fast, lest you fall."

"I daresay you are right," Hermione acknowledged a trifle breathlessly. "But as the danger is past, kindly return me to my seat in the barouche."

"As you wish." Dismounting, Grandison lifted her off his horse and saw her settled against the squabs inside her elegant carriage. Only then did he take the liberty of seizing her trembling hand and planting a kiss on her wrist, above her glove.

Awe-struck, Hermione gazed at the Irishman and then at her hand. Isabella noted the ardent gleam in his dark eyes before he turned to remount. Eager to catch her aunt's reaction, she shifted her gaze just in time to see the lady's gloved fingertips flutter distractedly up to her throat. Then, as if suddenly aware of Isabella's curious stare, Hermione made a concerted effort to regain her composure.

"You know my niece of course, but I don't believe you've met Lady Lansbury and her daughter, Fanny."

Grandison wrested his gaze from Lady Ponsonby's pale countenance and rose-tinged cheeks. Controlling his mount's ill-timed urge to dance, he bowed toward the landaulette. "Charmed, Lady Lansbury. Servant, Miss Lansbury."

Fanny murmured a polite response before

renewing her search for her brother. Squinting into the sun, she said, "I've spotted the phaeton's yellow wheels. Look sharp, Mama! Jon's coming round again."

"Mercy!" Lady Lansbury lamented. "What with the driver pushing his chestnuts to breakneck pace, however shall I contrive to catch Jon's attention?"

Grandison scowled into the sun. "Is Lansbury your cub, ma'am?"

"Yes, he's my eldest," Amanda conceded with a distracted smile, the bulk of her attention upon the approaching phaeton.

"Do you wish me to intercept him?"

"That would be splendid."

"Say no more. I'm on my way."

Grandison proceeded to maneuver his horse directly into the path of the high-perch phaeton. Isabella caught her aunt's sharp intake of breath just before she saw the sporty carriage barreling toward the Irishman at a neck or nothing speed.

"Archie!" Isabella squealed.

Both hands busy subduing his rearing chestnuts, Archie gave no sign he'd heard her astonished cry. His violent tug on the reins caused the precariously-balanced, high-perched phaeton to shimmy. Thwarted in their attempts to buck, the matched pair dug the heels of their hooves into the softly-packed dirt, braking to a gradual halt.

Minutes later, Isabella watched Archie

deftly sandwich the phaeton between the landaulette and the barouche. Then, as a sop to the proprieties, he paid his respects to Lady Ponsonby and allowed Jon to make him known to his mother and sister, before training twinkling gray eyes upon Isabella.

"Afternoon, Bella. Acquiring a little town bronze I make no doubt."

Butterflies danced in Isabella's stomach. Anxiously she searched his frank, open countenance, reassured by hints of good humor in his facial expression. Thanks be to God! she thought. He's no longer angry with me!

"Is the phaeton yours? Or is it a vehicle for hire?"

Archie gave a rueful chuckle. "It's mine all right and tight. Present from my godfather in honor of my twenty-fifth birthday."

"The Earl of Chandos? Since you're staying at his house, I assume you patched up your long-standing quarrel?"

"Yes. Excellent sport, my godfather! Not above giving a fellow a second chance," Archie averred as he shot her a pointed look.

At a loss as to how best to respond to his veiled barb, Isabella decided her best course was to keep her tongue between her teeth. Thus, her sense of ill-usage was compounded when, much to her dismay, Fanny said, "Jon's lucky to be your friend, Mr. Brainridge. I can't tell you how much I envy him your invitation to take a drive in your phaeton."

Archie's countenance bespoke wry amusement. "Minx! Shame on you, trying to cut the wheedle at your brother's expense."

Fanning flushed cheeks, Fanny persisted. "Could you not ask Jon to step down? While he and Mama converse, you could take me up in his stead."

"Mind your tongue, child!" Lady Lansbury admonished. "I'm sure you don't wish to disgust Mr. Brainridge by being too forward."

"Yes, Mama," Fanny replied, her small, piquant features suitably contrite. "I beg your pardon, sir. I should have waited for an invitation."

"Not at all. I'd be delighted to take you for a short drive, Miss Lansbury, provided your mama has no objection."

Fanny gave a happy shriek. "Do you truly mean it?"

"I'll have you know I'm a man of my word. Even if a certain female"— Archie's glance touched upon Isabella briefly before moving on— "chooses not to believe it. Hop down, Jon, and hand your sister up."

"Confound it, Archie, I'll thank you not to spoil Fanny. Highly unlikely she'll learn how to go on, if you insist upon rewarding her rag-manners."

"Cut line, Jon. It'd take more than a turn round the park to spoil her." Archie bowed his head in Lady Lansbury's direction. "With your permission of course, ma'am."

"Sir, are you certain your vehicle is safe for a gentlebred young lady?"

"I should never have issued the invitation if I thought there was the least risk."

Her ladyship smiled. "Brazen little hoyden. I vow she doesn't deserve such a treat, Mr. Brainridge."

"She apologized. Very prettily I might add."

"Very well. Fanny may accompany you for a short spin," Lady Lansbury relented.

A mute observer to the byplay, Isabella experienced a peculiar queasiness in the pit of her stomach. She stared at the retreating phaeton, totally oblivious to the desultory conversation between Jon and Malcolm Grandison and to the occasional verbal exchanges of the two noblewomen, comfortably ensconced in their respective carriages.

Consumed by jealousy, all Isabella knew was she'd like to wring Fanny's pretty neck! Archie's as well, she ruthlessly amended.

Hours later, composure restored, Isabella heard the strains of a concerto wafting from the music room as she paused at the top of the stairs. Fingertips tracing the sleek contours of the highly-polished teakwood banister, Isabella was conscious of the luxuriant contrast of cool satin against her warm skin as she negotiated her descent. Just as she reached the bottom step, her aunt struck a discordant note. It echoed and reechoed like a fading clap of thunder.

Only to be expected, Isabella supposed. Her ladyship had been blue deviled all through dinner. Come to think of it, she had been on edge ever since their afternoon drive in Hyde Park. Obviously Grandison's attentions had upset her. But were they actually unwelcome?

Isabella's brow puckered as she paused at the music room's entrance. In a sense, that gentleman had her sympathy. After all, what possible harm could come of a perfectly civil greeting in a public place? It was hardly his fault that Hermione had been pitched from the barouche. Nor was he to blame because her ladyship seemed to fear she was on the verge of succumbing to his ardor.

At times, Isabella wondered if her aunt knew her own mind. Perhaps it was not Malcolm Grandison she distrusted, but the fact that— almost against her will— she was drawn to him. It would certainly account for her skittishness whenever in his presence. Eager to solve the riddle, Isabella had tried to get her aunt to confide in her on more than one occasion— with no success. On the contrary, her gentle probes had only succeeded in making her aunt more evasive. But something was definitely amiss and Isabella was determined to get to the bottom of it.

"Do come in, dearest," Hermione coaxed.

Isabella sailed into the room, ostensibly anxious to receive her aunt's stamp of approval on the ivory satin gown ordered expressly for her debut at Almacks.

Lady Ponsonby's tight, set smile waxed genuine. "My dear, you look charming."

"Thank you. What were you playing as I wound down the stairs?"

"Herr Ludwig van Beethoven's Second Piano Concerto. Why?"

"Such a gloomy piece."

Hermione gave a dry chuckle. "The composer is German. A somber race on the whole."

"I dislike leaving you to face the evening alone while in the doldrums. Perhaps I should make my excuses to Lady Lansbury and keep you company."

"Has your common sense gone abegging? Nothing could offend the august patronesses more."

"As if I care a button what those social dragons think. You're much more important."

"Have a care, dearest. Society's good opinion matters. Particularly to an eligible young lady in her first season. Don't tease yourself on my account, child. Elsbeth will look after me. She's used to dealing with my moods."

"Very well. Since you insist, I shall go."

"There's a good girl! Did you enjoy our drive in the park this afternoon?"

"For the most part, yes." Isabella's forehead creased. "That reminds me. Aunt, I simply don't understand your aversion to Mr. Grandison."

"What makes you think I dislike him?"

"You poker up whenever he comes near you."

Hermione fixed her troubled gaze upon her niece. "I see I'll have to be more circumspect. Your eyes are too keen," she said crossly.

"There! What did I tell you? I knew there had to be a reason!"

Lady Ponsonby sighed. "Truth to tell, he's a common fortune hunter."

"A fortune hunter? Mr. Grandison?"

"What else am I to think? His antipathy toward me began the minute he laid eyes on me when my husband brought me to Ireland as a new bride. I don't think Robert ever realized his bosom bow disliked me, else he'd never have appointed him as one of the trustees of his estate."

"Maybe Grandison had a change of heart. He seems very fond of you now."

Hermione sighed. "No doubt you've noticed I'm drawn to the blackguard as a moth to flame. I can only be glad he never bothered to hide his contempt for me during my marriage. Without that insight into his true character, it would be so easy to succumb to his potent Irish charm.''

"You've a right to your suspicions, but I fail to see why his marked attentions to you since your husband's death make you assume he's a fortune hunter.''

"Horse breeding is a precarious undertaking. I suspect he's overextended. Only consider he was never one of my admirers. Yet ever since Robert died, he fawns over me like some besotted fop. Well, he doesn't fool me for a minute. He's after my money.''

"If true, what a pity he doesn't have the sense to love you for yourself alone!''

"Put in that light, perhaps he is right to despise me,'' her aunt responded. "I fear I'm a sorry case, Isabella.''

''Fiddlesticks!''

In response to a slight commotion in the hallway, Hermione conjured up a brittle smile. "Your loyalty to me does you credit, even though I fear it's sadly misplaced. Run along, child. It will never do to keep Amanda waiting.''

How unfortunate that Aunt Hermione took such a cynical view of Malcolm Grandison's suit, Isabella thought, as she allowed a footman to assist her into the Lansbury carriage. As they journeyed to Almacks, Isabella— still annoyed with Fanny for flirting with Archie that afternoon— replied to her attempts at conversation with monosyllables, and soon found herself free to resume her ruminations.

Before her aunt had taken her into her confidence, Isabella had been all set to encourage a romance between Aunt Hermione and Malcolm Grandison. Such a course of action was now out of the question. More's the pity, Isabella lamented, firmly convinced her aunt was too young, and too beautiful, to resign herself to permanent widowhood.

Nine

A post chaise drew up to the curb. Messrs. Brainridge and Lansbury scrambled down the hastily lowered steps. "Ugly ain't it?" Jon asked, with a nod at the building before them.

Archie glanced at the unprepossessing structure. "Dare I hope its interior is an improvement?"

"Don't bank on it. The rooms are commonplace and the refreshments border on the intolerable."

"You're bamming me."

"No, I ain't."

"But, Jon, you gave me to understand that gaining entry at Almacks practically guarantees my acceptance by the *ton.*"

"Quite! The high-born patronesses guarding the entrance screen out the undesirables. Once those paragons deign to accept you, you'll have more social engagements than you care to attend."

"No wonder Chandos was so pleased that

you wangled me a voucher. Good of you to make such a fuss when I introduced you to him. Godfather's infirmities keep him house-bound much of the time and I suspect life gets a bit flat now and again."

A wide grin split Jon's face. "Don't be daft. Wouldn't have missed trading insults with the peppery old gent for anything! Besides, I've an ulterior motive for dragging you here tonight, so you can stubble your thanks."

"Oh? Care to enlighten me?"

"Concerns my sister."

"What, that taking little minx I met today in the park?"

"Who else but Fanny? Only got one sister. Thanks be to God!"

"That's neither here nor there. How may I serve you?"

"No way I could avoid showing up here tonight. Not after Mama gave me a trimming for neglecting my duty to Fanny this afternoon. So, faced with the prospect of having to dance attendance upon my sister, I decided I might as well wangle you a voucher. Kill two birds with one stone, so to speak."

"What am I then? Insurance you won't die of boredom?"

"Exactly!"

Archie flashed a lopsided grin. "I'm flattered you find me so amusing, old chap. I trust I won't disappoint you."

"Dash it all, that ain't what I mean. Truth is, I need a favor . . . or rather two favors."

Amiable by nature, Archie was surprised to find he was fast losing patience. "Jon, stop beating the devil about the bush and tell me what you want of me."

"Want you to dance with my sister. Mind you, our marked attention is no guarantee she'll take, but at least we can insure Fanny ain't mistaken for a curst wallflower."

"Lobcock! What a piece of work you make of a simple request! I'll be happy to dance with your sister. And the other favor?"

Jon flushed. "Before Mama threw a spoke in the wheel, I'd engaged to play cards with a few chaps at a private establishment. Hate to let them down on such short notice. But if I were to slip away early, leaving you behind to do the pretty, I daresay Mama will be none the wiser."

Archie's gray eyes narrowed marginally. "Happy to be of service, but have a care at the card table. Never do to get in too deep."

"No need to worry on that head. Discovered a new method of winning at hazard. Eager to put it to the test." In a burst of gratitude, Jon clapped Archie on the back so vigorously, his friend winced. "Knew I could count on you in a pinch. Once inside I'll introduce you to Lady Jersey, so dust off your manners."

Having survived a vetting by the obstreperous countess— sardonically dubbed Silence by her peers— Archie wasted no time approaching Jon's sister. He was not too surprised to find her surrounded by prospective beaux. However, Bella's circle of admirers cut up his peace to such a degree, it was difficult to curb his envy as he led Fanny into the set just forming.

"You appear to have a great many admirers, Miss Lansbury."

She nodded complacently. "Only because I'm not the least interested in bringing any of them up to scratch."

"You don't plan to marry?" Archie asked, intrigued.

"Nothing so drastic. I simply don't wish to fix my affections quickly. For if I don't receive any suitable offers, I'm sure to wangle a second season from Papa."

"Your stratagems amaze me, Miss Lansbury."

"I'm only seventeen. Too young to be thinking seriously of marriage."

"How refreshingly original of you! And what of your friend, Miss Cox? Does she share your aversion to holy wedlock?"

"I've no idea. Surely you know her mind better than I do. After all, you've known her longer, have you not?"

"Yes, since she was in leading strings, but I don't pretend to understand her. To hear

*A*llow us to proposition you in a most provocative way.

Say Yes to 4 Free Books!

COMPLETE AND RETURN THE ORDER CARD TO RECEIVE THIS $16.47 VALUE. **ABSOLUTELY FREE.**

(If the certificate is missing below, write to: Zebra Home Subscription Service, Inc., 120 Brighton Road, P.O. Box 5214, Clifton, New Jersey 07015-5214

4 FREE BOOKS

Yes! Please send me 4 Zebra Regency Romances without cost or obligation. I understand that each month thereafter I will be able to preview 4 new Regency Romances FREE for 10 days. Then, if I should decide to keep them, I will pay the money-saving preferred subscriber's price of just $13.20 for all 4...that's a savings of over $3 off the publisher's price. (A nominal shipping and handling charge of $1.50 per shipment will be added.) I may return any shipment within 10 days and owe nothing, and I may cancel this subscription at any time. My 4 FREE books will be mine to keep in any case.

Name _____

Address _____ Apt. _____

City _____ State_____ Zip_____

Telephone ( )_____

Signature _____   RP0495
(If under 18, parent or guardian must sign.)

Terms and prices subject to change. Orders subject to acceptance by Zebra Home Subscription Service, Inc.

AFFIX
STAMP
HERE

ZEBRA HOME SUBSCRIPTION SERVICE, INC.

120 BRIGHTON ROAD

P.O. BOX 5214

CLIFTON, NEW JERSEY 07015-5214

her talk, making her bow to society went sorely against the grain."

A faint scowl disturbed Fanny's creamy brow. "Now that you mention it, she was reluctant to make her come-out, but her aunt insisted."

Archie grimaced. "She's surrounded by admirers. No doubt she enjoys their attentions."

"What female wouldn't! But Bella's nobody's fool. She's well aware that the majority of men dangling after her think she's an heiress."

"That's ridiculous! She has no dowry."

"I know. She told me. It's a mystery how such a wicked rumor ever got started."

A bitter laugh escaped him. Fortune hunters hot on her trail. One more complication to deal with. Archie flushed. No wonder she'd turned down his latest offer. Bella regarded him as a penniless gamester. Perhaps she thought he was after the money she was rumored to inherit, too. Lord, what a coil!

Actually nothing could be further from the truth. Once wed, Archie stood to inherit his godfather's vast fortune. Pity he couldn't tell Bella how things stood, but he had given his word.

"Poor Bella. From ragamuffin to alleged heiress. Thank goodness, I had the good sense to pay my addresses to her when she didn't have a groat to her name."

"She refused you, Mr. Brainridge? I must own I'm surprised."

"Bella turned me down as a consequence of my misspent youth. I was a gamester, you see, and she doesn't believe I've reformed."

"Have you truly changed?" Fanny peered earnestly into his face.

"Indeed, I have! Unfortunately, I'm having the devil's own time convincing Bella."

"Don't be downcast. She may change her mind."

"What makes you say that?"

"She's been cross as crabs ever since you took me for a spin in the park. If you ask me, she's jealous."

Archie's countenance brightened. "Miss Lansbury, do you truly think Isabella has a *tendre* for me?"

"Absolutely!"

"You give me hope."

Fanny sobered. "But if you care for Bella, why didn't you ask her to dance first? Are you deliberately trying to fan her jealousy to fever pitch? If so, I beg you to desist. I would remind you that we share the same coach, and I'd liefer not have her slit my throat on the way home."

"Minx! I plan to begin mending my fences the instant I deliver you back to your mama for safekeeping."

Unhappily for Archie, by the time he'd worked up the courage to request a dance,

Isabella was in a rare taking. Tilting her chin at a defiant angle, she assured him with feigned sweetness that her dance card was already filled. Knowing Bella, he had expected fireworks, but for her to dissemble was outside of enough! Who did she think she was trying to bamboozle? Some green halfling?

"Let me see." He took a firm grip on her wrist and was scanning her dance card before she was aware of his intention.

"What a bouncer!" he exclaimed. "You've two dances free."

Isabella snatched back her card. "Archie, take a damper. Those are waltzes. No young lady in her first season is allowed to waltz at Almacks."

"Ha! Of all the brummish stories, that takes the palm!"

"I'm not roasting you. Ask Lady Lansbury, if you don't believe me."

Archie cocked his head in her ladyship's direction.

"Isabella speaks the truth, Mr. Brainridge," said Lady Lansbury. "A young lady in her first season isn't permitted to waltz unless given leave by one of the patronesses."

"Miss Lansbury has a few open spaces on her card. Why not dance with her?" Isabella said snippily, once Fanny had been led off by her partner to form the next set.

Archie's eyes darted to Lady Lansbury,

worried she had overheard Isabella's catty remark, but fortunately, her ladyship's attention had been claimed by another matron.

He leaned toward Isabella and said, "If I didn't know better, I'd think you were jealous."

Color high, she squeaked indignantly. "Jealous? Me?"

"Yes, you, my love. Fanny's an engaging brat, but I prefer to dance with you. God knows why!"

"Archibald Brainridge, I'm warning you, if you know what's good for you, you'll give me wide berth."

He chuckled softly. "You terrify me, sweetheart."

An hour later, he nursed a glass of orgeat, beyond a doubt one of the worst concoctions he had ever tasted. A quadrille was in progress and he was able to watch Isabella, dancing with her partner, without drawing undue attention.

Viewed with hindsight, it had been rash to lead Fanny out on the dance floor before first requesting that Bella stand up with him, but he had been eager to perform the small service Jon had requested.

Besides, Archie could think of no better way to test a theory fomenting in his brain ever since their chance encounter that afternoon in Hyde Park. For it was there he had received the first inkling that Isabella—

whether she cared to admit it or not— might actually love him. Why else would the troublesome baggage be jealous of Fanny? A silly smile flitted across his broad countenance as a comforting warmth spread through every vein in his body.

He sobered. If that were the case, why had Bella rejected him? Why could she not understand that she was the only female he wished to marry? Dammit! He was tired of being in her bad books. While earlier it had seemed like a good idea to make her jealous by paying court to Fanny, Archie now regretted his childish impulse. Indeed, unless he thought of something quick, the evening would end before he managed to soothe Bella's ruffled feathers.

By George, he had it! A look of unholy glee suffused his appealingly-open features. Ridding himself of the unsavory glass of orgeat, he wove purposely through the crowded room in search of Sally Jersey.

A short time later, Isabella was startled to see Archie approaching. How dare he continue to badger her! Only belatedly did she realize he was escorting Lady Jersey. What was he up to now?

"Good evening, Miss Cox. I've caught glimpses of you dancing with various partners. Enjoying yourself, I trust?" the loquacious patroness inquired.

Endeavoring to keep tight rein on her rising temper, Isabella dropped her ladyship a curtsy.

"Mr. Brainridge has prevailed upon me to allow you to waltz. I've come to tell you personally. You have my permission."

Isabella did not want to dance with Archie, but dared not risk offending the powerful patroness. Not that she cared if she became a social pariah, but the Lansburys might suffer and that she could not bear.

"Before this eligible young blade spirits you off, I beg you to inform Lady Ponsonby of my intention to call."

"I . . . I would be most happy to convey your message to my aunt, your ladyship."

"Dear Hermione," Lady Jersey mused, a glint of good-natured malice in her eyes, "it's been an age since we've had a comfortable coze."

"Come, Bella, I believe this is our dance."

Isabella lifted her gaze until her blue eyes met Archie's gray. She had half a mind to balk, but thought the better of it as his strong supple frame loomed directly before her, blotting out everyone else. His arm was extended toward her expectantly and there was a quiet watchful look on his countenance.

Another spurt of rebellion surfaced but quickly died as she caught sight of the tender glow in his gray eyes. Against her better judgment, she went willingly into his arms. A combination of the appealing music, the intimacy of the embrace, his clean, masculine scent and the proximity of his hard firmness to her softness wove a web of enchantment. There's something intoxicating about waltzing in the arms of your beloved, she decided as they whirled. Then all thought ceased and her senses took over. Isabella closed her eyes and surrendered herself to Archie's arms and the strains of the waltz.

Mind floating in a frothy haze, she savored these precious moments as though they were rare pearls. But all too soon, a sudden chill at the small of her back caused a barely perceptible shiver. With a poignant sense of loss, she realized Archie's warm hand had rested in that precise spot and was now gone. Furthermore the music had ceased. Her eyes flew open, alarm registering in their sapphire depths.

Rueful resignation dominated Archie's gray eyes as he said huskily, "I don't want to move either, sweetheart. But the next set is forming. To linger any longer in the middle of the floor is bound to set tongues wagging."

Suiting his actions to his words, he took a step backward. Bella swayed. He braced her firmly by the shoulders until she caught her balance.

"Thank you," she whispered. "I feel a trifle lightheaded."

"All that whirling makes one dizzy. Care for a cool drink?"

Isabella's nod was all the impetus Archie needed. Tucking her arm protectively in his, he conveyed her into a small anteroom that housed the refreshment table.

"Lemonade or orgeat? Take your pick."

"Lemonade."

"Ready to return to the ballroom?" he asked once they'd quenched their thirst.

Bella glanced wistfully about the deserted anteroom. "Could we linger here a few more minutes before returning to the mad crush of the ballroom?"

Archie hesitated. "Nothing I'd like more than to oblige you, my dear. However, the gentlemanly thing to do is to deliver you to your chaperone before our absence causes comment."

Isabella made a small, unladylike snort. "Gammon! I've known you since you were in shortcoats. Since when have you ever behaved like a gentleman?"

Watching the familiar laugh lines crinkle at the corners of his eyes, Isabella's heart swelled. One of Archie's most endearing traits was his sunny nature. When particularly amused, even his eyes smiled.

"Little termagant!" he chided affectionately. "Never miss a chance to rip me up, I vow! Very well, my love. Against my better judgment I've decided to indulge your whim."

My love? Heart racing, Isabella gave an inward sigh. She knew better than to allow Archie to address her so warmly. The trouble was the endearment floated into her eardrums like liquid velvet.

Suddenly self-conscious, she said, "You are right. Lingering here is not all the thing. We'd best go back before my absence starts tongues wagging."

Flashing a rougish grin, Archie deftly maneuvered Bella to the far side of a potted aspidistra. "In a minute, my love. I mean to steal a kiss first."

Isabella stiffened. "Here where anyone may walk in? You wouldn't dare."

"Oh wouldn't I?"

Rising to the challenge, his head swooped down and his lips claimed hers. She twisted and squirmed, but he held her fast.

Then her treacherous lips parted involuntarily and Archie swallowed her cry of protest as his tongue invaded the sweet, moist cavern of her mouth. Just as she had become caught up in the delicious sensuousness of the waltz, Bella ceased to struggle as she became helplessly ensnared in myriad sensations of the seemingly endless kiss.

Considering how she had fought to avoid the intimacy, she felt curiously let down when he called a voluntary halt to the proceeding.

"I owe you an apology. I oughtn't to have kissed you— especially not here."

"Indeed, I resent being treated like a trollop!"

"Lord, Bella, I'm sorry. It ain't that I don't respect you, but I'm having the devil's own time keeping my hands off you, sweetheart. And you're so curst obstinate, you make it impossible for me to pay my addresses to you properly."

Isabella's eyes flashed. "So I'm to blame, am I?"

"No, you ain't. Not by a long shot. I simply want to say my intentions are honorable and I love you to distraction. More to the point, your jealousy of Fanny gives me hope that you love me."

"Why, you conceited coxcomb! How dare you presume to know my mind?"

"Not your mind, my love, your heart. You love me, Bella. You're just too stubborn to admit it. But make no mistake, I intend to wed you, Isabella Cox, come hell or high water."

Ten

"Mercy! Where have you been, child?" Lady Lansbury asked as Archie delivered Isabella to her chaperone.

"Enjoying a glass of lemonade in the refreshment room, your ladyship. Bella was thirsty."

Lady Lansbury eyed Archie's bland countenance before training her troubled gaze upon her young charge's flushed face. "What a whisker! I saw neither of you there when I peeked in a few moments ago."

Archie looked chagrined. "I fear we were standing on the other side of the aspidistra, ma'am."

"Were you indeed? Young man, I suggest you take yourself off, before my temper gets the best of me."

"Before I do, allow me to apologize for any distress I inadvertently caused." He bent low over her hand.

"Sorry to put you in a worry, ma'am," Isabella said contritely once Archie had withdrawn.

"Perhaps I was a little too hard on Mr. Brainridge, but I'd never forgive myself if your reputation came under a cloud due to my negligence."

"I quite understand. Next time, I shall inform you of my intention before deserting the ballroom."

"Next time, I hope you will give a thought to the disappointment of your subsequent dance partners."

"Quite right, ma'am. I promise I shall."

Lady Lansbury looked nonplussed. "My word, Mr. Grandison seems to be headed in our direction."

Isabella giggled. "Mayhap he means to set you up as his latest flirt."

"Fustian! It's plain as a pikestaff that he has a *tendre* for Hermione."

"I fear my aunt does not return his regard."

"Pity. Hermie stands in need of a strong protector."

"She'd never pick him. She thinks he's a fortune hunter after her money."

"Nonsense. The man's head over heels in love with her. Furthermore," Lady Lansbury whispered behind her fan, "if the tattlebaskets have their facts right, he recently inherited a comfortable fortune from a distant cousin who migrated to the West Indies."

"An interesting tidbit, if true, ma'am," Isabella admitted.

"I consider my source impeccable. It may be wise to drop a hint in Hermione's ear," Lady Lansbury observed as the object of their conversation halted before them.

"I beg your indulgence, ma'am." Grandison addressed Lady Lansbury after a creditable bow. "It's imperative that I speak to Miss Cox in private."

Amanda Lansbury cast him a look of reproval. "It's not in my power to grant you leave, sir. Whatever you wish to say to Miss Cox will have to be said in my presence."

The Irishman's swarthy skin darkened. "So be it! I wish Miss Cox to convey a message to Lady Ponsonby." He shifted his gaze to Isabella. "Forgive my want of tact but my watch is missing."

Lady Lansbury gasped. Feeling out of her depth, Isabella's eyes darted from one to the other.

"Your watch, sir?"

"Aye, my pocket watch. I was wearing it when I stopped to chat with your aunt this afternoon in the park. You may have seen it dangling from my waistcoat pocket."

She had seen it! The nape of Isabella's neck prickled with apprehension. "I collect it's turned up missing?"

"It has," he averred, grim-faced.

Lady Lansbury whispered, "God save us!"

What an odd thing for her to say! Isabella thought. But she had no time to ponder—not with Grandison acting the bully. Mustering her waning courage, Isabella forced herself to look him square in the eye.

"Indeed, sir, I am sorry to hear of your loss."

"Cut line!" he barked, his dark eyes cynical. "Just be sure to tell your aunt I mean to call and warn her to not be so birdwitted as to deny me."

Sketching a perfunctory bow, he strode off. Isabella, still puzzled by her chaperone's unhealthy pallor, studied her ladyship's countenance in the hope of divining the cause.

"Pray don't stare at me, child!"

"Your pardon, ma'am. That odious man seems to hold Aunt Hermione responsible for the loss of his watch. Did you ever hear such nonsense?"

Lady Lansbury gave a faint moan and blanched a shade paler. Suspicions piqued, Isabella said, "There's more to this than meets the eye, isn't there?"

"I fear so."

"Tell me."

"I cannot. It's not my place. Ask your aunt."

Isabella's head spun. Extraordinary! Lady Lansbury seemed to think her friend had appropriated Grandison's watch. Which was ridiculous. Or was it? After all, when her aunt had toppled from the coach, she had wound up in that gentleman's lap. Isabella's palms began to sweat as she recalled her aunt's quarrel with Elsbeth over the diamond pendant while shopping in Bond Street. But surely she was jumping to groundless conclusions, Isabella reasoned. Surely Aunt Hermione was blameless. After all, what possible use would she have for a man's pocket watch? Even assuming she coveted it, she could well afford to buy as many watches as she wished. No it couldn't be true. Aunt Hermione was not a thief. Isabella vowed to erase such an unworthy notion from her mind. The idea was patently absurd.

Isabella's reverie was broken by Fanny's return on the arm of her dance partner, who promptly withdrew.

"Mr. Westrop tromped on my flounce, Mama. Whatever shall I do?"

Her ladyship gave a languid shrug. "You've two choices, my love. Either march up to the ladies' retiring room and mend it or direct me to summon the carriage."

"I'd be happy to help you pin it up, Fanny," Isabella volunteered.

"Does your offer mean you are no longer out of charity with me, Bella?" Fanny asked.

"It does. Come along, pet."

Isabella linked her arm with Fanny's who smiled at her and said, "I only flirted with Mr. Brainridge because I had my heart set on a ride in his new phaeton. I had no idea he was your beau. Do forgive me."

"You're forgiven. Now hush."

"You've no cause to be jealous," Fanny persisted as they sailed into the ladies' cloak room. "He's besotted with you, Bella."

"Poppycock!"

"No, it's true. Why else would he spend the entire drive plying me with questions about you?"

Why else, indeed, Isabella mused, spirits soaring until recollection of Malcolm Grandison's ominous threat sent them plummeting back to earth. Odious man! No wonder her aunt did not like him. Poor Aunt Hermione. What a taking she would fly into when Isabella relayed his message! Yet Isabella had no choice but to do as he bade, for it would be far worse for her aunt to receive him with no prior warning.

An instant after Isabella and Fanny returned to the ballroom, Archie strode to her side. "Waltz with me, Bella?"

While they waited for the orchestra to strike the first note, she longed to surround herself to the anticipated joy of dancing a second waltz with Archie, but was too worried about her aunt to relax. The very recollection of Grandison's barbed remarks made her shiver.

"What's troubling you, Bella?"

"Nothing important."

"Goose! Something has you tied up in knots. Tell me."

"I shouldn't know where to start. Anyway, it's pure conjecture on my part. I've no proof."

"Suppose you let me be the judge of that."

Isabella slanted a probing glance at him through her lashes. "If I confide in you, will you promise not to tell anyone else?"

"I promise. Quit stalling, Bella. You can trust me."

"Very well. It's a muddled tale at best, but here goes."

She quickly sketched a picture of her aunt's reclusive way of life, touching on the incident at the shops, and ending her account with Grandison's insinuations in regard to his missing watch.

"Furthermore, I think Lady Lansbury considers the message he charged me to deliver is a veiled threat and I agree."

"It does sound like something havey-cavey's afoot." The orchestra began to play softly. "On the other hand, it could all be a bag of moonshine."

"Do you actually believe I want to think my aunt's a pickpocket? Why do you think I'm in such a fidget? Oh, Archie, whatever shall I do?"

"Don't fret, sweetheart. There has to be a way to come about. Let me think."

He led her into a waltz that proved so

lively, it made them both breathless. Thus, it was not until the dance ended that he spoke again. "Can you ride with me in the park tomorrow morning?"

"I suppose I can. Aunt doesn't have any prime-goers in her stable, but I trust her groom can find me a respectable mount. But really, Archie, this is no time to be making an assignation."

"Don't be daft. Mind you, it's probably all a hum, but for Lord's sake, Bella, if you happen to run across that curst watch, bring it with you. I'll meet you at Hyde Park corner at seven o'clock sharp."

"Assuming I deliver it into your hands, what then?"

"I shall attempt to return it to its rightful owner with none the wiser."

"Archie, you're a trump!" Isabella exclaimed, her eyes shining.

"Knew you'd get around to appreciating me sooner or later," Archie grumbled. "Now, hush, sweetheart. I have to deliver you back to Lady Lansbury's care, and it'd never do to tip our hand."

"Is my aunt still up, Symonds?" Isabella asked the elderly retainer upon entering the town house in Berkeley Square.

"I believe she has retired, miss," the butler

responded as he bolted the front door behind her.

How vexing! She would have to wait until morning to confront her aunt.

"Is the matter urgent, Miss Isabella?"

"Er . . . no. Nothing that won't keep."

But climbing the stairs, it occurred to her that she could not afford to wait. If her aunt had Grandison's watch in her possession, Isabella must get hold of it tonight. There would be no time tomorrow. Not when she must meet Archie at the park so early.

Pausing before the door of her aunt's boudoir, she could detect no splash of candlelight filtering under the door or around its edges. Nor did she hear anyone moving about inside. Symonds was right. Aunt Hermione had retired for the night. Isabella was tempted to slip inside and begin her search immediately but it would never do to be caught snooping and there were servants still milling about. Just the idea of how humiliating it would be if she were discovered going through her aunt's things made her shudder. Plagued by misgivings, she continued her preamble down the hall and into her bedchamber.

Her abigail had nodded off in a wing chair while awaiting Isabella's return from Almacks. Reaching down, Isabella gently shook her.

"Daisy, wake up."

"Oh it's you, miss. Must have dozed off." Yawning, the maid tottered to her feet.

"I hated to wake you, but I cannot scramble out of this gown without your help."

"No, indeed, miss, not with all those tiny buttons down the back."

As soon as the maid had assisted her mistress into a nightgown, she was sent off to bed.

Isabella spent the next half hour pacing the floor, trying not to fret over what she must accomplish once certain all the servants were abed. By the time she deemed it was safe to pick up a candle and pad down the hall, her nerves were stretched so taut she feared they might snap.

Drawing to a halt in front of her aunt's door, Isabella took a deep, fortifying breath. Before her courage failed, her hand closed over the knob. The squeal of an unoiled hinge as the door swung inward made her cringe. Her heart stopped, then its normal beats accelerated alarmingly when she sighted a shadowy apparition looming in the doorway. Scared witless, Isabella nearly dropped the flickering candle. As the ghostly form surged toward her, panic clawed a jagged trail up her spine. Isabella opened her mouth to scream, but clogged vocal chords prevented her from making a sound.

The murky figure pushed Isabella ruthlessly backward, pursuing her into the hall.

Candlelight wobbled crazily as the ghostly form took shape. "Elsbeth! You scared me so badly I almost jumped out of my skin."

"Have a care with that taper, miss," the abigail cautioned. "Now then, suppose you explain what you're up to."

"I must speak to my aunt at once. The matter's urgent."

"I don't advise waking her. She finally fell asleep after suffering a bad case of hysterics earlier."

"Very well, I shan't wake her. But there's something in there I need. Let me pass. I'll be quiet as a church mouse, I promise."

"I must speak to you first. Though not here in the hall where we might be overheard."

"Come then. We can talk in my bedchamber."

No more was said until they reached their destination. Noting Elsbeth's wan pallor, Isabella insisted she be seated and catch her breath before unburdening herself.

"I don't know where to begin," the abigail wailed.

"Begin with my aunt. Are you certain she's asleep?"

Elsbeth nodded. "Finally. But earlier she had such a violent attack of the vapors I was forced to dose her with laudanum."

"Oh? Does she fly into these hysterical fits often?"

"No, miss. Only when she—" The abigail broke off with a strangled cry. "When under great stress, she's not herself, you understand, and sometimes she . . ."

"Prigs some nobleman's watch?"

Elsbeth stared at Isabella. "How long have you known?"

Isabella sighed. "Only a few hours. Imagine my surprise at Almacks when Mr. Grandison sauntered up to me and practically accused her of stealing his watch this afternoon in Hyde Park. By the by, he wished me to tell her he plans to pay her a call."

The abigail dabbed at her eyes. "To press his suit no doubt. The blackguard! He knows she does not wish to remarry. She came up to London to escape his attentions. All for naught since he would follow."

"All things considered, it's preferable to Newgate," Isabella observed dryly.

"If only I could have prevailed upon her ladyship to remain secluded upon her country estate."

"Stay in Ireland? But why?"

"The quieter environment is more soothing to her temperament and when she's content she's less likely to . . . to . . ."

"Steal?"

Elsbeth looked pained. "Must you state the matter so baldly?"

"If you know of a gentler way to say my

aunt's a common thief, I pray you will tell me."

"How can you be so unfeeling when she's been so kind to you?"

Isabella lowered her gaze, ashamed of her churlish outburst. "I beg your pardon. It's been . . . such a shock."

"Her ladyship's a helpless victim of a troublesome sickness. But despite her inability to curb her deplorable tendency to be er . . . light-fingered, she's safer in the country where everyone dotes on her and both the local gentry and the shopkeepers tolerate her weakness."

"You're bamming me!"

"No, miss. It's the Gospel truth. It all began early in the marriage when her ladyship suffered a miscarriage and was told she would never bear a living child. My lady went into a decline and for a time I feared for her sanity, but then she seemed to recover. However, during the next London season, a dreadful scandal loomed on the horizon. But his lordship made restitution and retired with her to his country estate. He was a wonderful husband. Lord Ponsonby never made a fuss when a local tradesman dunned him for some trinket that had caught her ladyship's fancy. Indeed, on the one occasion a member of their social circle turned up on his doorstep to beg the return of a family heirloom, no one was quicker to oblige."

"I'm glad you've confided in me, Elsbeth. It makes me understand my aunt better. However, what we must decide immediately is how we can save her from the consequences of today's ill-considered impulse."

"If only Lord Ponsonby were still here to shield her. I fear Mr. Grandison means to use her transgression to gain his objective."

"That's blackmail."

"Aye, but she has no choice but to bend to his will."

"I quite agree marriage is preferable to prison or being transported, but I've a plan that may answer. Mind you, it's risky, but considering the alternatives, it's worth a try."

"Excellent! But before you explain it, I'd like to apologize for trying to drive a wedge between her ladyship and yourself when you first arrived. I confess I was worried you'd be disgusted, should you learn your aunt's secret. However, it didn't take me long to realize your heart's in the right place."

"No need to go on, Elsbeth, I quite understand."

"You mentioned a plan," she prompted.

"So I did. Archibald Brainridge is a particular friend of mine. We plan to meet in the park early tomorrow morning, ostensibly to go horseback riding. However, if I'm able to bring him the watch, he will endeavor to return it before Grandison can make good his threat to call upon my aunt and badger her into marrying him."

"Mr. Brainridge seems open and above-board, but are you certain you can trust him?"

"Yes, I am. We grew up together, you see, and he's used to rescuing me from scrapes."

Elsbeth rose. "I'll fetch the watch."

Eleven

Early the following morning, Archie and
Isabella enjoyed a brisk canter in Hyde Park.
Afterward, he rode with her back to the
mews behind her aunt's town house where
he helped her dismount. It was here that she
handed over Malcolm Grandison's pocket
watch and said, "Funny thing. Up until that
minute Elsbeth brought it to me, I kept hoping she was innocent."

Archie studied Isabella carefully. The distress he heard in her voice unsettled him.
Worse, just before she'd lowered her gaze, he
had glimpsed disillusionment warring with
embarrassment in the depths of her sapphire
blue eyes. Archie blinked rapidly. He wanted
to gather her close and shield her from further hurt but she looked so tense— so brittle—
he was afraid if he touched her she might
shatter into a million pieces.

So instead, he took hasty leave of her and
went to meet Jon Lansbury at Jim Jackson's,
where he stood just inside the entrance of

the famed boxing salon, trying to think how best to proceed.

Jon regarded his friend with open suspicion. "Whatever you're up to, Archie, it's too smoky by half."

"Damn your eyes, Jon! Bella's embroiled up to her pretty ears in a devilish coil and I'm determined to help her come about. But if you're too chicken-hearted to lend me a hand, then take yourself off."

"Humph! Fine way to treat a friend."

Archie sighed. "Right. I've no call to rake you over the coals. My apologies."

"Oh, stubble it! What can I do to help?"

"I've something that belongs to Grandison. It's imperative I return it to him without his knowledge."

"By jove, you plan to slum-guzzle the Irishman."

"I'm going to try. Are you with me, Jon?"

"Of a certainty! Nothing I relish more than a bit of a challenge."

Archie clapped his friend on the back. "Good show," he said, then shifted his gaze back to the two men engaged in a friendly sparring match inside a roped-off ring.

"At the moment it appears Gentleman Jim commands Grandison's whole attention. Should that situation change, can I count on you to create a diversion?"

"Of course. But how do you propose to

return the article without being seen?" Jon asked.

"I've no time to explain. Just do your part. There's a friend!"

Careful to keep to the dimly-lit shadows, Archie stole inch by painstaking inch up to the chair where the Irishman had left his upper garments before climbing into the ring. Eying the dancing fighters, Archie waited until Grandison's back faced him before he slid the gold watch into the upper pocket of the Irishman's waistcoat.

Then, as swiftly as he could manage without arousing suspicion, he retreated.

"All right and tight?" Jon murmured from the corner of his mouth when Archie joined him at ringside.

Archie shot him a cat's-in-the-creampot smile.

Jon grinned. "That's the ticket!"

"Steady, old chum," Archie cautioned. "Eyes front."

"Quite," Jon agreed.

Archie trained his gaze upon the boxers. Eyes widening, he held his breath. The match was over! He used his handkerchief to blot tiny droplets of perspiration dotting his forehead. He'd almost been caught red-handed!

The Irishman climbed through the ropes. Jon and Archie bowed and said in unison, "Servant, sir."

"Top of the morning to you, lads," he boomed as he strode past them.

Archie's body felt as tense as a wound whipcord. He'd willingly part with a coach wheel in order to see the look on Grandison's face when he discovered the missing gold watch tucked in his waistcoat pocket. Yet Archie dare not track Grandison's progress— lest he give himself away. Instead, he steeled himself for the inevitable repercussions as he watched Gentleman Jim exit the ring with his usual lithe grace.

Archie did not have a long wait.

"Devil a bit," Grandison roared. "Brainridge and Lansbury, I'll have a word with you."

Jon slanted a speaking look at his crony. Archie responded with a warning frown.

"Dammit, I said come here! Or are you both too hen-hearted to confront me?"

The fat's well and truly in the fire, Archie silently acknowledged once he faced the irate gentlemen. "Something got your wind up, sir?" he asked, careful to keep his expression bland.

"You returned my watch, didn't you, Brainridge? How dare you meddle in my affairs? I've a good mind to tip you a settler."

"Before we come to blows, may I point out you don't have a particle of proof."

"Archie's right, you don't, sir," Jon said loyally.

The Irishman's swarthy face darkened ominously. "Maybe not, but I'll lay odds you did."

Archie shrugged. "I'm not a betting man. Pity."

"If you think I'll let you make a jackass out of me, you're sadly mistaken!"

Like a crazed bull, Grandison lunged. Happily for Archie's hide, the ever-nimble Gentleman Jim grabbed hold of the irate Irishman and held fast.

"Unhand me, mon. I've a score to settle."

"Not in my establishment you don't," the famed boxer retorted, before training his flinty gaze upon Archie and Jon. "If you young cawkers haven't made yourself scarce by the time I count to three, you'll have me to deal with. One . . ."

Gentleman Jim's count was interrupted by Grandison's enraged bellow. "You've done me an ill turn, Brainridge. Rest assured, I intend to even the score."

"Two . . ."

"Coming, Jon?" Archie inquired.

"Most assuredly."

Whoever said discretion was the better part of valor knew what he was talking about, Archie decided, timing his exit so that he passed through the outer door as Gentleman Jim called, "Three."

* * *

At the Ponsonby home in Berkeley Square, Daisy guided her young mistress's arm into the sleeve of a tan, kerseymere spencer worn over a walking dress of brown poplin. Someone scratched the bedchamber door from the hall side.

Isabella called permission to enter. When Elsbeth walked in, Isabella dismissed Daisy, who promptly withdrew.

"Home from your morning ride, miss?"

"Yes, all is in train."

"Splendid. Your aunt is blue-deviled today. She needs cheering up."

"Very well. I'll join her shortly."

Elsbeth hesitated, then plunged on. "Don't be shocked if she has no recollection of yesterday's misstep. She often forgets past indiscretions."

"Really? How can she possibly?"

"The mind has strange facets. Perhaps it's a blessing she's able to blank it out for the most part."

Isabella didn't know what to think as she followed Elsbeth out of the room and down the hall where she tapped lightly on her aunt's door.

"Come in," called Lady Ponsonby from within.

Isabella entered to find her aunt propped up in bed, a breakfast tray across her lap.

Taking note of Isabella's walking dress,

she said, "My dear, Bella, where are you bound so early?"

As Hermione paused to take a tentative sip of chocolate, Isabella stifled an urge to laugh. It was going on eleven o'clock. How ironic that, while her aunt slept peacefully, she'd risen at dawn in order to meet Archie in Hyde Park and give him the purloined pocket watch . . . a watch that apparently her aunt no longer recalled stealing.

"To Hookham's, ma'am. Fanny's meeting me there. Why? Do you wish to come?"

Smiling, her aunt shook her head. "I'm feeling lazy today. And since I don't expect any callers, there's no reason for me to dress until midafternoon."

"Gracious! I almost forgot. Lady Jersey may pay you a call."

"Sally Jersey? You must have windmills in your head."

"No, ma'am. She asked me to give you advance warning of her intention."

Fear mingled with anticipation in her ladyship's green-brown gaze. "In that case, I must take particular care with my toilet. Ring for Elsbeth, dear."

She hastened to do her aunt's bidding. While they waited for her aunt's dresser to appear, Isabella awarded her ladyship a fond smile, tinged with sadness occasioned by the realization that, from this day forward, she must keep close watch on her aunt's conduct.

Indeed, it was almost as if their roles were reversed and she were the guardian and Aunt Hermione the child.

"I must be off else Fanny is liable to fly into a fidget," said Isabella the instant Elsbeth joined them.

"Have a good time child. Don't give a thought to your poor aunt squirming under the sharp eyes of Lady Jersey."

"Do you wish me to stay and bear you company?"

"No, I was only teasing. Enjoy your outing but send back the carriage for me just before two. I mean to visit Clarimonde's. A new bonnet is just the thing to shake off my megrims." Her hazel eyes narrowed thoughtfully. "I've a marvelous notion! Meet me at the milliner's. I've a fancy to treat you to a new bonnet!"

"Aunt, really . . . there's no need. You've already been much too generous."

"Fiddle! I don't propose to argue. You wouldn't be so cruel as to deny me the pleasure, would you?"

Her niece gave a burst of exasperated laughter. "Very well, Aunt, I shall meet you there at half-past two."

It was only when she reached the anteroom belowstairs that Isabella recalled Malcolm Grandison's professed intention to call upon her aunt. Not that he would be inclined to make good his threat, provided Archie's plan met with success. Nevertheless, Isabella took the precaution of instructing Symonds to deny Grandison entry, should he present his card.

Shortly after four that same afternoon, Lady Ponsonby emerged from the elegant milliner's shop encumbered with three hat boxes. Despite the hustle and bustle of street traffic, she managed to catch her coachman's eye. Correctly interpreting her signal, he dispatched a lanky young footman to take the hat boxes from his mistress as well as the two carried by her niece, who'd now joined her aunt at the curb.

Reaching her ladyship's side, the footman struggled to shield her and her young charge from the crush of passersby on the painfully narrow pavement. His task was complicated by a crotchety old gentleman, who had the gall to demand, "Out of my way, you silly females!"

Isabella peeked round the corner of one of the stacked hatboxes. The cantankerous old goat was shored up on one side by the aid of a cane of highly-polished hickory. His other side was kept firmly upright by a sturdy male companion, whose face was blocked from her line of vision by the cumbersome hat boxes.

Once the elderly crosspatch realized that

neither female intended to obey, he shook his cane at Lady Ponsonby and said, "Clear out of my way, you frivolous creature! No doubt, madam, you've been busy spending some long-suffering mate's blunt on feminine fripperies!"

Incensed, Hermione starched up her diminutive frame until she gave off the aura of a haughty queen. "How dare you use that tone with me, sir!"

Undaunted, the crusty old gentleman had the temerity to brandish his cane a second time. Thrown off balance, he tottered and nearly lost his footing— not to mention almost pulling the younger man, who still clutched his other arm, down to the pavement with him. Fortunately for the old man's brittle bones, his stalwart companion somehow managed to keep them both on their feet.

"Brazen wench!" the old gentleman exclaimed, obviously vexed by Hermione's continued refusal to step aside. "How dare you defy me?"

"Sir, I promise you I shall not stir one inch until you apologize for your rude, overbearing manner," Lady Ponsonby informed him in a glacial tone.

"Apologize! Me? What a hubble-bubble creature you are, madam!"

Hazel eyes flashing with defiance, her ladyship took revenge by standing firm and fixing the peppery old coot with a withering stare.

At the onset of the brangle, Isabella's vision was constricted. However, once her aunt's footman managed to relieve her of the cumbersome hatboxes, her perspective improved dramatically.

"Archie!" she cried.

"God almighty! Bella!" he responded, equally startled.

"Good lord! Never say you're acquainted with these troublesome females."

"I fear so, sir," Archie admitted with a rueful grin.

"Damn your eyes! Why didn't you say so?"

"Too busy trying to keep you from foundering, sir."

All lapsed into an awkward silence. Like a frozen tableau, no one moved with the sole exception of the footman, who nimbly bore the five hat boxes off to the waiting carriage.

The crotchety nobleman gave a roar of laughter. "If that don't beat all hollow!" His cackle grew as his sense of humor assuaged his anger. "I collect I've made a regular Jack pudding of myself. Well, don't just stand there. Introduce me."

"Not until you apologize, sir," Archie said firmly but without heat.

The Earl of Chandos's keen eyes raked his grandnephew's face. Gradually the expression in the old man's gaze subtly altered to emit a glimmer of respect.

"You'll do, lad, you'll do," he said. His eyes darted to Lady Ponsonby. Somehow he managed a shaky bow. "Madam, my sincere apologies. I hope you will forgive this corkbrained old fool!"

"How can I refuse to honor such a handsome apology?" her ladyship responded graciously.

"My lady, as you've probably already surmised, this crabby relic beside me is my godfather, the Earl of Chandos."

"My pleasure, sir," Hermione said, dipping a curtsy.

"Uncle, the young lady is Miss Isabella Cox, whom I've known from the cradle, and the stylish matron, you almost came to cuffs with, is her aunt, Lady Ponsonby."

Quite soon after introductions were dispensed with, the irritated grumblings of pedestrians—forced to skirt the foursome by stepping into the gutter—made it abundantly apparent they were blocking traffic.

"We appear to have created a bottleneck," Archie observed. "Prudence dictates our swift removal from this congested spot."

"There's a confectioner's only steps away," her ladyship hinted.

"Famous!" the earl exclaimed. "Come, my beauties. Let us repair to this establishment with all due haste. My rickety bones cry out for a sitdown."

A short time later, all four were comfortably seated in Windsor chairs, sipping cups of India tea. Isabella nibbled a biscuit selected from a silver tray that rested upon a linen covered table.

"You're a country-bred lass, Miss Cox?" the aged earl asked, after blowing on his tea to cool it.

"Yes."

"First trip up to London?"

"I imagine that's all too obvious," Isabella said ruefully. "I did hope by now to have acquired a little town polish."

The earl cackled. "Rest easy, miss. Though you've retained a modicum of frankness I find vastly appealing, there's no doubt your gown is all the crack."

The delicate pink in Isabella's cheeks deepened, as she demurely lowered her lashes. "It's all my aunt's doing. She's spared no expense to fit me out in elegant style. I've tried to tell her I've no need for such an extensive wardrobe as it can only lead to a false impression of my true situation, but she refuses to listen."

The earl cocked an attentive ear. "I must confess you've piqued my curiosity, Miss Cox. What, pray tell, is your true situation?"

She sighed. "That of a poor relation. You see, my father gambled away my dowry. When he died, a distant male cousin inherited Cox Manor. I count myself lucky Aunt Hermione took me in, even though she insisted I make my bow to society."

"But of course I did. I hope I know my duty," averred Lady Ponsonby, boldly interrupting the *tete-a-tete* between Isabella and the earl.

Seconds later, Archie called her ladyship's attention to a raven-haired beauty seated at the opposite side of the room. "Ma'am, judging from Lady Jersey's gestures, she wishes you to join her at her table."

Hermione glanced across the room, then struggled to her feet. "She did send word of her intention to call. I suppose I ought to see what she wants."

Rising, Archie crooked an elbow. "Allow me to escort you, ma'am."

As Lady Ponsonby and Archie moved out of earshot, the earl favored Isabella with a benevolent smile. "I've lost track of our conversation. Where were we, child?"

"We were discussing my aunt's insistence that I have a season."

"So we were. I daresay you brighten many a ballroom, my dear. Why not enjoy your good fortune while you may?"

"I would except for the false impression it creates that I'm hanging out for a husband. However, I think the matter is slowly correcting itself, since lately I've noticed a slight thinning in the ranks of my admirers."

"I gather the fortune hunters are seeking greener pastures."

Isabella giggled. "The joke's on them, sir. My aunt is an heiress with a very warm fortune, not I."

"And how is my nephew faring with this season's crop of eligible young ladies?"

"As to that, I couldn't say, my lord."

"Perhaps you would be so kind as to keep an eye on him as a special favor to me."

"Me, sir?"

"I'd be forever in your debt. You see, I'm anxious to see him buckled before I cock up my toes."

Isabella felt flustered and slightly disgruntled. Though admittedly leery of wedding Archie herself, the thought of him marrying someone else was unexpectedly painful. She gave herself a brisk shake. Such a dog in the manger attitude would not do.

"I should like to oblige you, my lord, but I fear I'm too well acquainted with his weakness for cards to recommend him to some green girl."

"No such thing. Did he not tell you, he's given up gaming?"

"He told me, but I'm not ready to believe it. Although I will own that, as far as I know, he's curtailed his gambling since my father died. I must confess Papa was not a good influence on Archie."

"Your candor does you credit. I begin to understand why Archie is so fond of you, my dear. I collect, both being motherless chicks, you were thrown together a lot as children."

"Quite."

"I realize it's a grave impertinence on my part to broach such a delicate topic, but, precisely why, child, did you reject Archibald's offer?"

Isabella felt ready to sink with embarrassment. Her hands flew to cover her burning cheeks. "Sir, I'd no idea he confides in you."

"I wormed it out of him. Why did you refuse him?"

"Setting aside my aversion to marrying a gamester, I've no money, nor does Archie. It's not that I aspire to great riches, you understand, but I should not like to think of my children in want."

"Didn't the lobcock tell you I've settled his debts and made him an allowance?"

"No, he didn't. Though of course I noticed his new wardrobe. But even if he's not virtually penniless, what's to say he doesn't resume old habits?"

"Because he has a new passion— one worthier of his talents, I might add."

"A new passion, sir? I fear I don't understand."

"You know of course that Archie's father quit Brainridge Hall last year to take up residence at the large estate he recently inherited in Leicester."

At Isabella's nod, the earl warmed to his subject. "Nonetheless, I gather you've no inkling that before he left he appointed Archie the baliff of Brainridge Hall."

Isabella's eyes widened. "Archie, sir? Indeed, I'd no idea."

"So I thought." Chandos gave a gleeful cackle. "More to the point, I'm proud to say the innovative farming methods he's introduced since he took charge have resulted in the estate showing a profit for the first time in memory."

Isabella felt terrible. Obviously, she'd been wearing blinders. "I hardly know what to say. I've ever been fond of Archie. It pains me that I've misjudged him so badly."

The earl patted her hand sympathetically. "No need to fret, child. We all make mistakes."

Isabella considered this for a moment then said, "I daresay you are right, sir. Mine was allowing my prejudice against gaming to blind me to Archie's true character."

Chandos's wizened countenance sobered. "As to your fear that the lad won't stray back to the gaming tables sometime in the future, that, of course, cannot be guaranteed. However, if nothing else, the passage of years tends to make even the silliest clodpole wiser. In a way, all security is an illusion that can vanish in a wink. Life entails taking chances, my dear. While I agree with you it is only prudent to avoid an addiction to cards and other forms of frivolous gambling, especially for ruinously high stakes, in a higher sense, life, itself, is a gamble."

Isabella's face lit in a shy, slow smile of heightened understanding. "What you say is true, sir. What a pea-goose I am not to have realized it before this."

"Mind you, Archie's allowance is just adequate. He cannot afford many luxuries. I would not spoil him, you understand."

"Your attitude does you credit, my lord."

"My child, I hope you will reflect on what I've said. If you decide to throw in your lot with Archibald, I don't think he'll let you down."

"I promise to think it over, sir. Archie is lucky to have you to guide him. I'm glad you two have reconciled."

"So am I, my dear. He's a good lad, as you'll find out for yourself, should you decide to go the distance." The earl had no sooner closed his mouth when, out of the corner of his eye, he saw that Lady Ponsonby and his greatnephew were about to rejoin them. While Archie helped her ladyship resettle herself in her chair, the earl winked and said to Isabella, "Now if you'll excuse me, I'd best have a word with your aunt before she takes me to task for neglecting her."

Lady Ponsonby smiled at Chandos as he turned to face her. "I feel I must correct my niece's erroneous impression that she is a penniless waif. Naturally, I plan to settle a handsome sum upon her when she marries."

"Good gracious, Aunt, there's no need. You've done more than enough for me already."

"Allow me to be the judge of that, young lady." The sternness in her aunt's face softened. "I should have discussed the matter with you early on, but frankly I assumed you knew my intention."

"No, indeed. I never dreamed you planned to be so generous."

"Why not, pray tell? I can well afford it and I've grown quite fond of you. Stands to reason that I'd wish to see you comfortably settled."

"I hardly know what to say, ma'am."

"Say thank you and have done, child!" Rubbing his hands together, the earl trained his beady eyes upon Lady Ponsonby. "I find your niece an engaging chit. Mind you don't spoil her."

Hermione beamed. "Impossible, sir! Isabella has too much common sense."

At this juncture, Archie deemed it prudent to interrupt. "It's time we took our leave. Uncle seldom leaves his residence in Grosvenor Square as even short excursions tire him. May I escort you ladies to your coach?"

As Archie assisted her to her feet, Isabella recalled Mr. Grandison's watch.

"The small commission I charged you with. Did everything go according to plan?"

Archie laughed. "By jove it did. Matter's taken care of all right and tight."

Isabella touched his sleeve and said in a soft undertone, "How can I ever thank you for the risk you took?"

With a devilish twinkle in his gray eyes, Archie cocked his head to one side and said, "Rest assured, sweetheart, I'll think of something."

Twelve

"Your servant, Lady Lansbury," Archie said, sketching a bow at yet another of the interminable balls given during any given London season.

"Good evening, Mr. Brainridge. Are you looking for Jon?"

"Our paths already crossed. Not in the sunniest of moods tonight, is he?"

"Very true!" Lady Lansbury responded. "Jon fancies himself in love with Miss Smollet. She recently became engaged to the Duke of Bevon."

Archie gave a bark of laughter. "No wonder he nearly bit my head off."

"He's the picture of absurdity, is he not? Making a cake of himself by standing on the outskirts of the ballroom and glaring at the schoolroom miss who has scorned him for another."

"Puppy love, ma'am. Jon will come about."

Looking harried, Lady Lansbury fanned herself vigorously. "If only I could be certain of that! To be honest, it's not just his wearing the willow that worries me. He insists upon wearing the stick pin Great-aunt Seraphina willed him wherever he goes— which includes those gambling hells he frequents."

Archie frowned. Truth be told, he'd been envious of the flawless diamond winking from the folds of Jon's pristine neckcloth when they'd spoken earlier. "I fear the sharpers have marked him as a pigeon ripe for plucking. I've tried to warn him, but he refuses to listen."

"Indeed, Jon has always been stubborn to a fault. I'm thinking of writing his father, though I dread the resulting kickup."

"Perhaps you should, ma'am. Meantime, I'll keep an eye on Jon."

"Are you certain you don't mind? I shouldn't like to impose."

"Gammon! Jon's my best friend. I'm not about to let the gull gropers sink their talons into him if I can help it."

"That's very kind of you, Mr. Brainridge. Especially after I was so short with you for keeping Isabella overlong inside the ante-room housing the refreshments at Almacks."

"I took no offense, ma'am."

"Did you not? I presumed you had when you stopped showing up at the same affairs to dance attendance upon her."

"Godfather caught a putrid cold. At his age, the consequences can be grave, so I kept close to his bedside until his health took an upturn."

"Indeed, I'm delighted to hear of his recovery."

"No more than I, ma'am." After a slight pause, Archie continued, "I don't see Bella. Didn't she accompany you this evening?"

"No, she's coming later. Thanks to Sally Jersey's prodding, Lady Ponsonby has decided to reenter society. Naturally she wishes to play chaperone to Isabella."

A pensive frown ruffled Archie's forehead. "All things considered, I wonder if that's wise."

Lady Lansbury tossed him a shrewd look. "Who can say? I am hoping for the best." Her facial expression became animated. "La, Hermie and Isabella have arrived."

"So they have. Excuse me, ma'am."

Archie stepped to Isabella's side just as she left the receiving line. "Evening, Bella. May I scribble my name on your dance card?"

She handed it to him. "It's good to see a friendly face in this crush."

"Miss me, did you?"

"A little," she admitted.

Actually, she had missed him a lot. Yet, perhaps it was for the best that she'd had this interlude to sort out her feelings. Lord Chandos had given her excellent advice. Archie had more backbone than her father. Since he had taken a solemn vow not to gamble it was ungenerous of her to doubt him.

"The mixed bouquet you sent was lovely."

Archie grinned. "Glad you liked it."

"And thanks for your note advising me of the earl's illness. I assume he's on the mend?"

"Indeed, he's as feisty as ever. Which reminds me, the calf's liver jelly you sent round made quite an impression."

Archie choked back a laugh as he wrote his name beside two waltzes. Never would he forget the look of loathing on his godfather's face when he had viewed the dubious treat.

"Indeed. So nourishing for an invalid, don't you agree?"

Archie tactfully changed the subject. "Speaking of Chandos, you're first oars with him."

Isabella laughed. "For all his crochets, he's a wonderful old humbug."

"I'm partial to the wily old gent myself," he admitted as he led her onto the dance floor. "Even though he's fast becoming a dead bore on the subject of matrimony."

"He just wants to see you settled," Isabella said primly as she assumed the proper stance.

"Patience was never his long suit. He can't understand why it's taking me so long to persuade the filly I've got my eye on to toss her bonnet over the windmill."

A delicate pink flush stole into Isabella's cheeks. "Oh? Did he offer you any advice?"

Mischief glimmered in his gray eyes. "Indeed, he's very free with that. Claims you need a push and it's up to me to provide it."

"Mayhap, he's right."

Archie tightened his hold on Isabella's waist. He peered down at her . . . wanting to believe . . . not quite daring to trust his own ears. "Wh—what did you say, sweetheart?"

The color in Isabella's cheeks deepened. "Pray don't regard my immodest tongue. I fear it quite literally has put me to the blush."

Heart drumming wildly, Archie screwed up his courage to the sticking point. "Dare I hope, you've had a change of heart?"

"No, never that!" cried Isabella.

The joyous triumph radiating from Archie's countenance faded and the corners of his mouth assumed a bitter twist. "For a moment there I thought my persistence was about to be awarded. Once again I'm mistaken."

Isabella stared at him, dismayed. She had sought to please him. Instead, she had hurt his feelings.

"Pointless to continue this farce." He stopped dancing abruptly. "Come, I'll return you to your aunt."

"No, please—not in the middle of the waltz!"

Gray eyes flinty, he resumed dancing. Isabella cut a furtive glance at Archie's face. His normally open features appeared frozen behind a cynical mask. A sharp wave of despair assailed her. Grain by grain, happiness was slipping away from her like particles of wet sand being sucked into a bottomless eddy.

"You misunderstood me. Please, you must listen!"

Archie regarded her warily. "You have my attention. Go on."

Fighting a rush of shyness, Isabella said quietly, "My fondness for you never waned. If anything it's stronger than ever. Why I've changed is my mind— not my heart. It's ever been constant."

Isabella had assumed that Archie would be pleased by her confession. Indeed, she had hoped his jubilation would shatter the almost unbearable tension that coiled like a taut snake ready to spring. Instead, he scowled at her, filling her with disquiet.

What if he had only been toying with her? How foolish of her to let down her guard— to confess that she cared for him? Isabella flushed, so embarrassed she wanted to die.

Indeed, she was so busy nursing her grievances, Archie's lighthearted chuckle barely registered.

"Abominable baggage! To keep me hanging by a thread for months, and then to finally tell me you care for me in the middle of the dance floor is outside of enough!"

From a dark dungeon of despair, Isabella's spirits catapulted to new heights. "Is there no pleasing you, sir?"

"Oh, I'm pleased as Punch," he assured her with a playful leer. "Just a trifle impatient to get you alone so I can demonstrate."

Eying Isabella's crimson cheeks, Archie gave a crack of laughter as he led her into a series of whirls that left them both breathless by the time the waltz ended.

"Dare I suggest a short stroll in the garden?"

Isabella demurely lowered her lashes. "I could do with a breath of fresh air."

Archie's gaze warmed as he regarded his beloved. "I'll speak to your aunt in the morning, Bella."

As they skirted neatly trimmed shrubbery, he thought to ask, "By the by, how is she faring these days?"

"You mean since she's reentered society?"

"Yes."

"Splendidly," Isabella said brightly, then quickly sobered. "Nevertheless, I can't help but worry that something will occur to overset her."

Archie halted abruptly. How unlucky could he get? He'd been keeping an eye peeled for a spot where they might be private— mayhap share a kiss or two. And now this.

"What's the matter?" Isabella asked.

"Grandison's with your aunt. I don't relish crossing swords with him at a social gathering."

"I wish he'd leave her alone. He never fails to distress her."

"Does he? I wonder why."

"She's convinced he doesn't care a fig for her, only for her money even though Lady Lansbury insists he already commands a comfortable fortune."

"If true, it's possible his interest is sincere."

"Yes, though, according to my aunt, highly improbable."

"I see. Come, we'll go to her rescue."

When Isabella voiced no objection, Archie moved them within earshot in time to hear Grandison playfully chide, "My dear, Hermione, didn't your mother ever tell you it's rude to stare?"

"I wasn't staring. I was admiring your evening attire."

"A compliment, madam? Almost you unman me." He gave a dry chuckle. "Pity I left my gold watch at home. It just didn't look right with formal evening dress. Never mind. My ruby cufflinks may strike your fancy," he teased.

"Sir, your conduct is infamous!" Archie cried. "Stop baiting her, else I shall be forced to call you out."

"Meddling again, Brainridge?" The Irishman threw him a look of disdain. "Pity I don't accept challenges from puppies barely dry behind the ears."

"Gentlemen, stop this senseless bickering at once!" cried Hermione. "I'll not have my niece and me made a laughingstock by the two of you snarling at each other like two mongrels fighting over a bone."

Archie hesitated, touched by the dismay mirrored in his beloved's eyes. But his self esteem was at stake. There was no going back. Grandison felt he had done him an ill turn and would never be satisfied until he was given the chance to even the score.

"Not quite a puppy, sir. I recently turned five and twenty," Archie said quietly.

Grandison opened his mouth to respond, but before he could, Hermione gripped his arm and said in a voice trembling with emotion, "If you continue this madness, I vow never to speak to you again as long as I live!"

Grandison peered at the soft hand clutching his sleeve and then up into Hermione's imploring hazel eyes. A ghost of a smile twitched at the corners of his mouth as he deftly peeled off the elbow length evening glove and proceeded to kiss her fingertips one by one. Time seemed to freeze as he lowered her hand with infinite slowness, his dark eyes brimming with passion as he continued to study her face.

"Brainridge, this is neither the time nor the place to settle our differences. Our conduct has troubled the ladies. We must beg their pardon."

"I couldn't agree more, sir. Ladies, my apologies."

Once the tension had eased, Lady Ponsonby cast Archie a look that brooked no argument. "Kindly oblige me, Mr. Brainridge, by escorting my niece back inside before her absence causes comment."

"Certainly. But first, may I have your permission to call on you tomorrow morning?"

"But of course."

"Thank you, my lady. Come, Bella."

Isabella hesitated. "Are you certain you will be all right, Aunt?" She glanced pointedly at Lady Ponsonby's escort.

Grandison gave a short bitter laugh. "Sheath your claws, kitten. I promise not to harm a hair on your aunt's head."

"I've no reason to trust your word, sir," Isabella said tartly.

"True, however, you appear to trust Brainridge. Rest assured should I dare play fast and loose with her ladyship, your stalwart defender will be certain to call me to book."

"Do go with Mr. Brainridge, dearest," Lady Ponsonby said. "I promise you I'm in no danger."

Archie's gaze darted from Lady Ponsonby to Grandison. He concluded there was more to their tenuous relationship than he'd originally supposed.

"Yes, come along, Bella," he commanded, determined to override any lingering qualms. But to his mild amazement, she allowed him to guide her back inside without a murmur.

Soon after, Grandison restored Lady Ponsonby to the ballroom and took his leave.

Too tense to sleep after handing Isabella and her aunt into the barouche and bidding them goodnight, Archie decided to drop in at White's, hoping a bit of male camaraderie would relax him. He half expected Jon to hail him from one of the card tables until he recalled his friend's mention of a private engagement.

Although several gentlemen acknowledged his presence with a nod, Archie did not feel he knew anyone well enough to intrude. Since Jon was not there, perhaps he, too, should leave.

"Looking for me, Brainridge?" Grandison inquired.

Startled, Archie croaked. "No, sir."

"Prowling the nooks and crannies of White's in the wee hours is not your usual style, Brainridge. What brings you here tonight?"

"Lansbury, sir. His mother asked me to keep an eye on him."

"So she should! Silly jackanapes thinks he can run tame in the gambling hells that abound in the seamier sections."

"Good lord! I think the world of Jon. Can't have him end up in the basket, can I?"

"Your sense of loyalty is commendable. Will you join me in a glass of brandy, Brainridge?"

Archie's first impulse was to decline but since he had no idea where to begin to look for Jon and since he did not wish to discourage Grandison's friendly overture, he said, "A capital notion, sir."

The brandy arrived. Lounging in a velvet-covered wing chair, Archie took a cautious sip.

"Excellent vintage, sir."

"Pleased you approve," Grandison said dryly. His expression grew thoughtful. "I never see you seated at a card table. Why is that, I wonder?"

"I've sworn off gambling, sir."

"What? Not even a friendly wager on a sure thing?"

"Exactly, so."

Grandison tossed him a dubious look. "See here, boyo, you may think the sun rises and sets on Miss Isabella Cox, but it'll never do to let her lead you round with a ring in your nose."

"It was my decision alone to quit. Though lord knows I love her."

"Plan to get riveted, do you?"

"If she'll have me, yes."

"In that case, I shall expect to see the announcement in the Gazette any day soon." Grandison looked pensive. "What do you say we bury the hatchet, Brainridge? I admit I was annoyed with you for returning my watch. I planned to use it to pressure Hermione into marrying me. All's fair in love and war, hey what?"

"Fine with me. I bear you no grudge."

"Good! Here's my hand on it."

Handshake concluded, Grandison took a generous swig of brandy and confided with a rueful grin, "I'm beginning to think I've used the wrong tack with Lady Ponsonby."

"Indeed. Artful persuasion can work wonders, I collect."

Grandison sighed. "If only Hermione would learn to trust me. I've only her best interests at heart." He drained the last dregs of brandy from his glass and refilled it from the decanter the porter had left at his elbow. "More brandy, Brainridge?"

"Just a spot, sir."

The Irishman poured an inch of amber-colored liquor into his guest's glass. They sipped in companionable silence.

"Can you believe it, Brainridge?" Grandison asked finally. "Lady Ponsonby turned me down flat. You'd have thought I'd offered her a slip on the shoulder instead of marriage. Silly widgeon thinks I'm a fortune hunter. Not a word of truth in it, but there you are."

"Yet she seemed friendlier toward you this evening. Perhaps you can persuade her to change her mind."

"Perhaps. Always fancied her, though initially there was no question of showing my regard. Best friend's wife and all that. But after Robert died, I'd hoped . . ." He gave a cynical chuckle. "My own damned fault she's skeptical now that I'm finally free to court her. Deuced difficult smothering my feelings for years on end. Only way I could manage was to deliberately mask my passion by treating her with feigned contempt. Must be entering my dotage to think it'd be easy to change her opinion of me now."

In an ebullient frame of mind, thanks to the brandy, Archie took it upon himself to try and shore up Grandison's sagging spirits.

"If I were you, sir, I'd be encouraged by the way her ladyship appealed to you when we nearly came to cuffs."

"By jove, you're right, Brainridge."

"If you exert a little patience, perhaps she'll come round to your way of thinking."

"Certainly worth a try," the Irishman concurred, his eyes narrowing pensively. "Hermione doesn't realize it but she's sailing too close to the edge."

"No question she needs a strong hand at

the helm, sir." Archie cocked his head to one side and grinned knowingly. "And unless I'm mistaken, you're just the man she needs to keep her on a steady course."

Thirteen

Isabella regarded the open archway that led into her aunt's drawing room with trepidation. Her heart beat as wildly as a trapped bird against her rib cage. And no wonder. In the next few minutes, her future would be decided.

So, why did she hesitate? Or did she still entertain doubts? True, Archie had vowed not to gamble, but what if he broke his word? Her faith in him would be shattered. On the other hand, he deserved a chance to prove himself, did he not?

Isabella drew a deep fortifying breath. No more dithering, she told herself firmly as she sailed into the room.

Lady Ponsonby beamed at her niece. "Dearest, Mr. Brainridge has come to pay his addresses and I've given my consent. Allow me to wish you happy."

Enveloped in her aunt's hug, Isabella heard Archie's dry chuckle. Embarrassed,

she stepped out of her aunt's embrace and
placed cold hands on hot cheeks.

"Auntie! Do hush!"

Hermione looked so guilty, Isabella almost
wished she had held her tongue. Before she
could think of a way to soothe things over,
her aunt excused herself on the pretext of
a crisis in the kitchen that must be dealt with
immediately.

Once they were alone, Archie saw Isabella
comfortably seated. Soberfaced, he regarded
her for a seeming eternity before a nervous
laugh escaped him.

"Frankly, my love, I don't fancy proposing
again on bended knee— unless of course your
heart is set on it."

Fortunately for Archie, sufficient time had
passed enabling Isabella to view his ill-fated
proposal at Cox Manor without rancor. Now,
however, despite his lighthearted tone, he
looked so anxious, her heart went out to
him. "Kneeling is not required," she assured
him with a wry smile.

"Will you marry me, sweetheart?"

"Yes."

Although she spoke in a thready whisper,
she knew he had heard her because he immediately drew her to her feet and coaxed
her to join him in dancing a jig.

Isabella was out of breath by the time they
stopped hopping about. She regarded Archie
with understandable wariness— wondering

what he'd take it his head to do next. His gray eyes gazed at her tenderly. *He's going to kiss me!* she realized. Her blood sang.

It was a very sweet caress, both chaste and fervent. It made her wish a kiss might be preserved like a favorite posy pressed between leaves of a book against the day one's spirits need a lift. Isabella touched her fingertips to her sensitized lips. Regrettably, a kiss was an intangible sensation too fleeting to be captured. Even so, she knew she'd always remember Archie's betrothal kiss with pardonable fondness.

Archie stood at ringside. A burly pugilist with cauliflower ears landed a punishing blow to Lansbury's midsection. It rocked Jon back on his heels. Archie winced.

Jon danced forward to deliver a combination punch that almost toppled his sparring partner. The corners of Archie's mouth curved skyward. Jon's timing and grace could not be faulted and, now that he had added science to his boxing skills, he was fast becoming a formidable opponent. Archie's affable grin faded. Pity, Jon's astuteness did not extend to the gaming tables. There, regrettably, night after night he continued to lose. Jon climbed through the ropes and joined Archie at the ringside. "Well, old chum, are you engaged to Miss Cox or not?"

Archie gave an exuberant chuckle. "You see before you the happiest of men."

"Congratulations." Jon clapped Archie on the back with such enthusiasm the latter's head reeled. "About tonight? Have you decided to join me?"

Archie stifled a sigh. The very last thing he desired was a tour of the gaming hells London had to offer. But he had promised Lady Lansbury he would look out for her son.

"Jon, I wish you'd see reason. If you don't quit gaming you face certain ruin."

"If I want a preacher to ring a peal over me, I'll find me one who's ordained."

Archie stiffened. "I meant no offense."

"I know you mean well, but frankly you're in danger of becoming a bloody nuisance."

Archie took another sip from the tankard of ale he'd been nursing all evening. He'd pointedly eschewed the gin offered gratis by the proprietors. In contrast, Jon had accepted every glass pressed upon him, which no doubt contributed to the singular lack of judgment he was displaying at the card table.

Glancing about, Archie understood why such places were called gaming hells. The room was crammed with perspiring men, who judged solely by their fetid odor had not bathed in a month of Sundays. It also reeked of stale tobacco and the sickly sweet smell of fermenting alcohol that made it hard not to gag.

To make matters worse, all the windows were covered in green baize— both to buffer the boisterous sounds of gamblers excited by the play and to shield those inside from the prying eyes of inquisitive passersby.

The closeness of the foul-smelling air compounded to Archie's discomfort. Beads of perspiration dotted his forehead. He blotted them with his handkerchief, though he was careful to keep a concerned eye fixed on Jon, who had been losing steadily for the last hour.

Truth be told, it was exceedingly difficult to remain an onlooker while his friend sank deeper and deeper into debt. Especially with Jon drinking gin— a concoction sardonically dubbed blue ruin because of the havoc it caused in the lives of the lower classes.

Archie's misgivings continued to mount. He suspected the deck in use at Jon's table was marked. Alas, he had no way of proving someone had fussed the cards— not unless he was able to examine them firsthand. Such a task would be simple if he took part in the play. But he could not— not without breaking his word to the earl and he was not about to do that. Especially not now that he had finally won Isabella's hand.

The Captain Sharp seated across from Jon

raised the stakes. Archie's frustration escalated. It seemed unfair that, while his own future now appeared rosy, Jon's circumstances seemed to worsen by the minute.

Once again Jon's adversary raised the limit. One by one the other players folded— all but Jon. Archie couldn't help but admire his tenacity.

Jon dug into his pockets and coming up short, asked, "Will you take my vowel?"

The card sharp lifted an eyebrow. "You have not as yet redeemed those from our previous session."

"The devil take you, I'm good for it!"

"No doubt. The question is when."

"As soon as my luck turns," Jon mumbled.

Despite the meager lighting, Archie could see the purplish flush that stole upward from Jon's neck until it completely suffused his face. Anxious to dispel the almost unbearable tension, Archie flashed a thick wad of pound notes. He counted off the exact amount needed to cover the bet.

"Here, Jon. Consider it a loan."

With a look of disdain, Jon batted Archie's extended hand aside. "Keep your blunt. I've something better!"

He undid the diamond stick pin fastened to his neckcloth and tossed it into the pot. A feverish gleam in his eyes, Jon insisted upon raising the limit.

Archie experienced a glimmer of hope.

Jon regarded the stick pin as something of a talisman. He would not risk it lightly. He must have a strong hand.

A minute later, Archie shook his head in disgust at the now-exposed cards. Granted Jon had held a good hand. The trouble was his opponent had a better one. Jon's shoulders slumped and Archie saw bleak despair in his eyes.

At first, Archie was only marginally aware of the fire burning in the pit of his stomach. Then suddenly he was furious with himself. Only a clunch stood meekly by while his friend was fleeced.

Adrenalin coursed through his veins. Archie yanked Jon off his chair and sternly ordered him to go home before he lost the clothes he stood in. Once his bemused friend had shambled off, Archie assumed the seat Jon had just vacated.

"Deal me in, gentlemen," he commanded.

The card sharp started to attach the diamond stick pin to his cravat, but Archie reached across the table and stayed his hand.

His gaze never wavered as he said coldly, "I'll stake my entire wad against the stick pin. Or are you too lily-livered to risk it?"

Clearly amused, the sharper said "Why not?"

"One card each, high card wins?"

His adversary returned the stick pin to the center of the table. "As you wish."

Archie tossed his notes on top. The card sharp scooped up the cards, shuffled them three times before he shoved the deck toward Archie and said, "Care to cut?"

Archie schooled his features to appear as if carved in stone as he made his selection. His eyes locked with the dealer's as he ran a deft finger around the edge of the card he had picked. He issued a cynical smile.

"This card's been shaved."

"Be demmed to you, sir! Are you accusing me of cheating?"

"I accuse you of nothing," Archie said evenly. "But the fact remains the deck is marked. I demand a fresh pack."

The card sharp's glare was so malevolent, Archie began to worry about covering his own back. Had he pushed the Captain Sharp seated opposite too far? he wondered. After all, he was a stranger here. For all he knew, everyone else in the room was a cheat.

To his infinite relief such was not the case. This he determined a minute later when the chap, seated to his right, noisily cleared his throat and said in a reasonable tone, "What he asks is within his rights. I suggest you break open a new deck."

Noting the difficulty the sharper had swallowing his fury, Archie's spirits lifted. Still in all, he knew he could not afford to grow smug— not if he was determined to win back what Jon had lost. Thus, it behooved him to keep a vigilant eye on his opponent as he shuffled the brand new set of cards.

"Cut?"

Archie divided the cards in two piles. The dealer deftly reassembled the deck, burned the first card and dealt Archie the second and himself the third, both face down.

Archie gazed into the steely eyes of the Captain Sharp opposite and then down at the card before him. He had to win back the diamond stick pin for Jon's sake. So much was riding on the luck of the draw. Would he win or lose?

Quelling a sigh, he gingerly lifted one corner of the face down card and hazarded a peek. His heart began to pound. *A king!* That was good. Very good in fact. The odds were in his favor. Only an ace could beat a king. Surely his opponent wouldn't be that lucky. Or would he?

The tension in the room was palpable as Archie flipped over his card.

"A king! He's won," an onlooker shouted.

"Not if the dealer has an ace," some doomsayer responded.

An argument broke out as to the odds against that contingency, but Archie refused to be distracted. He kept his eyes steadily fixed upon the card sharp. Thus, he was first to catch the man's wintry smile. Good lord! Was it possible his adversary had drawn the ace? Archie's heart plunged like a lead anchor straight down to his toes. What a gudgeon he had been to risk everything on the turn of a card. The suspense was terrible. *He had to know!*

"Turn it over, sir."

Gazes locked, the dealer flipped his card over.

"Another king!" someone shouted.

"A tie?" asked the sharper.

"No. First king wins," insisted a strident voice from the crowd.

A boisterous argument ensued. Roughly half of the onlookers insisted it was a tie while the rest claimed that the first king dealt had won the match. Archie longed to side with the latter, but since the point at issue had not been decided beforehand, his sense of honor would not permit him to do so.

"A tie, sir," he agreed. "Draw another two cards."

A glimmer of respect flickered so briefly in the sharper's eyes that Archie wondered if he had only imagined it. His opponent dealt Archie the top card and himself the next. Again, Archie lifted a corner. Damnation! A seven! With a pang of regret, he turned over the card.

"A seven. Bloody hell," remarked a disappointed onlooker.

Archie echoed the man's sentiments, though he allowed no hint of his discomfiture to show outwardly.

The dealer peeked at his own card. Observing his grin widen, Archie ruthlessly suppressed an urge to wipe that mocking smile off his opponent's face. What a fool he was! he mentally chastised himself. Once again he had wagered and lost. Would he never learn?

The card sharp shrugged, then flipped over his card.

"A three?" someone asked doubtfully.

"A three," another voice concurred.

"A three," said Archie, visibly stunned.

Pandemonium ensued. Archie took full advantage of it. Cool as ice, he scooped up the diamond stick pin and the pound notes he'd wagered and quit the premises.

The following day, bent on escaping a sudden, blinding influx of light, Archie burrowed his head deeper into the bedclothes. Despite his intention to achieve oblivion, small, niggling sounds kept intruding. The slide of drapery cords as they shuttled the window hangings aside to allow daylight to penetrate the bedchamber, for instance. Or Percy's mincing tread as he padded up to the carved, canopied bed and groped beneath the covers until he found Archie's shoulder and gave it a determined shake.

"Time to rise and shine, sir."

"Have a heart, Percy. Go away."

"Sir, you left strict orders to be awakened if you slept past noon."

"Damn your eyes, Percy! I've a devilish headache. If I issued such a maggoty command last night, I must have been a trifle castaway."

"You stayed up 'til dawn imbibing the earl's best cognac. By the time I tucked you in, you were as drunk as a brewer's horse."

Archie groaned. No wonder his head felt as if it were about to split wide open. "Leave me be, Percy. Let me sleep."

"Sleep won't cure your headache. If you can manage to sit up, I've a remedy for it."

With a martyred sigh, Archie threw back the covers, swung his legs over the side of the bed and sat up. The abrupt movement caused the hammering inside his skull to intensify.

"Here, drink this. It's already going on three o'clock and you promised to take your fiancee for a spin in your phaeton at five."

"My what? Have you gone queer in your toploft, Percy? I've no fiancee."

"That's not what you said when you returned from Berkeley Square yesterday afternoon and bade me to wish you happy."

"What? Do you claim I'm engaged to be married to Isabella Cox?"

Percy visibly stiffened. "I sincerely trust I've not been an unwitting party to one of your mad-brained hoaxes."

"What hoax? Talk sense, Percy. My head is pounding."

"Don't you recall telling me how pleased the earl was when you informed him that you'd obtained Lady Ponsonby's blessing and were now officially engaged to her niece? I shudder to think what the effect of learning it was all a hum will have on the venerable old gentleman's health."

Demeanor pensive, Archie studied the outraged countenance of his valet. Surely, even in his cups, he would not do anything so corkbrained. He was too curst fond of the peppery old nobleman to play him such a trick. Lord, how he wished the drumming inside his head would stop!

"To say nothing of the pain such a thoughtless prank will cause Miss Cox," Percy continued to scold. "She'll never forgive you for rendering her an object of pity amongst the *ton*. If only I hadn't obeyed your instructions to hand-carry the note you wrote to the *Gazette*."

"Devil take you, Percy. Are you saying I asked you to call round at the newspaper office with word of our betrothal?"

"I am. What's more, you threatened me to within an inch of my life if I didn't do as you bade."

This was dreadful. Archie was almost afraid to ask any more questions— yet he had to know. "Am I to understand notice of my engagement is printed in today's *Gazette*?"

Percy sniffed. "Read it for yourself, sir. You'll find this morning's edition on your breakfast tray."

The words were scarcely out of his valet's mouth before Archie snatched up the newspaper and began to thumb through it. Finding the announcement, he scanned it quickly. In a blinding flash, he now remembered proposing to Isabella yesterday and sealing her acceptance with a sweet kiss that had sent him into the alts and kept him there throughout the afternoon and early evening. He also recalled dining with his godfather and how happy the crusty old gentleman had been when informed of Bella's change of heart. From midnight on, however, his mind was still a blank. No matter. Since announcement of their engagement had been printed in the *Gazette*, they were now officially betrothed.

"I can't quite take it in, Percy. Even seeing it in print, it seems too good to be true."

"Then it's not a hoax?"

"Course it ain't. What kind of a paltry fellow do you think I am? No, I'm about to be leg-shackled all right and tight. Wish me happy, Percy."

"I already did, sir. Shortly before I took your note round to the newspaper."

Archie beamed. "So you did. Did I ever

tell you what a capital gentleman's gentleman you are, Percy?"

The corners of the valet's mouth shot upward. "Quit trying to throw the butterboat over my head, and drink this, sir."

Archie looked warily at the glass Percy was urging upon him. "What is it?"

"A tisane to take away your headache."

"Take it away. I ain't about to swallow a drop of that nasty-looking concoction."

Percy blithely ignored this outburst. "After you've downed it, I guarantee you'll feel better. By the by, did I mention Mr. Lansbury is in the drawing room awaiting your summons?"

Jon! In scattered bits and pieces Archie's recollection of the seedy gaming hell visited the night before came tumbling to the foreground of his mind. He glanced at his bedside table where he had left the stick pin and smiled. Jon would be delighted to get it back. Silly cawker loved flaunting his one good piece of jewelry. Why Jon had gone so far as to have the diamond appraised at Cartier's in Bond Street, where the owner himself had pronounced it flawless and offered to buy it for an astonishing sum. Jon had refused, supporting Archie's contention that he doted on the stick pin because he was sincerely attached to it— rather than because of its monetary worth.

Archie's eyes widened with alarm. Dear

God! He had reneged on his bargain with the earl. Granted Jon was his best friend, it still didn't excuse his own conduct. How could he have been so stupid as to gamble? He had worked so hard to earn Bella's trust. Now, he had lost her regard— forevermore!

Misery shone in his eyes. He had let the two people he loved most in the world down. Much as he shrank from breaking the old man's heart, he must tell him immediately. Godfather would disinherit him of course. Archie buried his face in his hands. Worst of all, he could no longer afford a wife. He would have to cry off.

"Sir, I beg leave to tell you, you are fast wearing out my patience. Drink this."

Archie spread his fingers far enough apart so that he could see his valet through the resulting slits. Percy's lips were pursed as if he'd just tasted something sour. He still held the dubious concoction.

"Hand it over," Archie ordered gruffly.

As he drained the glass, he almost wished it were hemlock. Indeed, it tasted so terrible, he fleetingly wondered if it could actually be hemlock. He gave a bitter laugh. At least if he had drunk poison, he would not have to face Bella and cry off. The last thing he desired was to break the engagement. But he must. Because, thanks to his own idiocy, he was once again a pauper. How Bella would despise him! Not that he blamed her. What he had done was despicable.

Already, his queasy stomach was settling down. Which meant he must now pay the piper. Archie handed the empty glass to his valet and gave a deep sigh. No, it was not hemlock he had swallowed, more was the pity!

Fourteen

Isabella peeked around the curve of the mahogany staircase at Archie who was pacing the marble floor of the entrance hall just below. She was in a bubbly, effervescent mood. Which was perfectly understandable. After all, she'd only recently discovered she was deeply in love. The expression in her eyes grew dreamy. Things could not be more perfect. Yesterday she had accepted Archie's offer. Today she had read the announcement of their engagement in the *Gazette* while sipping her morning chocolate.

Without warning, an icy shiver curled up her spine. Suppose she had never come to realize that she could trust Archie to keep his word? Fortunately, her conversation with Chandos had given her a fresh perspective. Thank goodness, she had come to recognize Archie's recent growth and to appreciate his strong sense of honor before it was too late.

Now, however, the future looked rosy. In just a few months, they were to be married.

Isabella hugged herself, so happy she feared she might burst. And this morning, Archie had promised to take her for a drive in his high perch phaeton with yellow wheels. It was a treat she had looked forward to ever since the day he had taken Fanny up beside him and left Isabella behind to choke in the carriage's dust.

She hazarded another peek at her intended as she began her descent. Archie's valet was to be commended. His master looked bang up to the mark in a Jean de Bry morning coat of olive green kerseymere worn with long breeches and top boots.

At the foot of the stairs, Isabella met Archie's unhurried inspection of her appearance with equanimity, confident that her new carriage dress of ecru jaconet worn over a peach-colored sarcenet slip was in the highest kick of fashion. His gaze lingered upon her wide-brimmed leghorn. The straw crown was ornamented with four rouleaux of peach-colored satin twined with white cord.

He flashed her a bemused smile. "My dear, you look enchanting."

Isabella felt as if she were floating. "I scarcely slept a wink," she confided. "I can't wait to ride in your phaeton."

Archie shot her an unguarded look. The misery she glimpsed in his eyes tugged at her heartstrings. Concerned, she touched his arm.

"What troubles you?"

"I must speak to you first." He glanced at the footman standing at rigid attention. "Is there somewhere where we be private?"

"Of course. Follow me."

She led him into a small sitting room. Once inside, Archie let go of her arm and made for the hearth where he stood with his feet planted firmly apart and his back to her. Isabella's mouth twitched at the corners. Was this what was meant by the cold shoulder? she wondered.

But her amusement was swiftly replaced with concern once she took note of his rigid posture. Something was wrong. But what? Only yesterday, he had proposed. Surely he had not grown tired of her already? Especially when he had been so persistent. Or was he the type who enjoyed the chase but who grew bored once the prize was within his grasp?

Isabella felt chilled to the bone. Something was very wrong.

"Archie, what is it?"

"I must tell you something and I don't know how best to go about it."

"You might try facing me," she said with a hint of acerbity.

Slowly, he turned around. "I want you to release me from our engagement."

His words struck home with the force of a painful blow. Deeply hurt, Isabella clamped a hand over her mouth barely in time to stifle an involuntary whimper.

"You want to cry off?"

"I have to."

"Why?"

"Last night I broke my vow."

"You gambled?"

"I . . . yes, I did."

"Oh, Archie, how could you?"

"I must admit I wasn't thinking straight. I know I let you down. Please forgive me."

No question she was disappointed. Yet she still loved him. A ray of hope took root. If he were willing to learn from his mistake, perhaps the relationship could be salvaged.

"What if I do? Do you think you'd be tempted to break your word yet again?"

"Last night was a special case— unlikely to be repeated. However, whether I'd weaken again is not the point. I've broken my bargain with Chandos. Once he cuts me adrift, I'll be in no position to marry."

"Don't be so hasty. With careful management, we can live tolerably well on the funds my aunt insists upon settling upon me."

"Forget it. I may be a pauper but I ain't about to become a leech. Do me a kindness. Cry off."

Isabella felt as if a great vise was slowly crushing the air from her lungs. "And if I refuse?"

"You must. I can't afford a wife."

"Nonetheless, I won't."

Isabella crossed her arms and hugged herself fiercely. Archie studied her blatantly defiant stance, then shrugged.

"You leave me no choice. If you won't cry off, then I must."

Isabella recoiled as if she'd been slapped. "But you cannot. It would be ungentlemanly. Only ladies have that perogative."

"Who says I'm a gentleman?"

The man was infuriating! Isabella decided. "Why you . . . you . . ."

"Bounder?" Archie asked.

"Exactly so!"

On her high ropes, Isabella scarcely noted Archie's parting bow. But the instant he left the room she missed him. Surely if he had lingered something would have occurred to mend the breach.

She heard the wheels of his carriage as it moved along the cobblestones and rushed to the window. Struggling to overcome her severely-dashed spirits, Isabella watched the phaeton turn the corner at the top of the street.

A tear splashed her bare arm. She had so looked forward to showing off her smart new ensemble during their drive in the park. Not only had Archie forgotten all about his promise to take her for a spin in his phaeton, the loathsome blackguard seemed determined to break their engagement.

Another tear splashed her skin. How could

she have been so foolish as to entrust her heart to someone as pigheaded as Archibald Brainridge?

Isabella stamped her foot. She was no milk and water miss content to pass through life in spinsterhood wearing the willow for her chuckleheaded suitor. She must do something before Archie's resolve hardened. The question was what?

For a seeming eon, she stood very still, her forehead furrowed as she concentrated. Then her brow cleared and her countenance came alive as she saw a bright spot on the horizon.

An hour later, the Earl of Chandos urged, "Have another apricot tart, my dear."

"No thank you, sir," Isabella demurred.

"Can't begin to tell you how pleased I am that you took a notion to call. Though it goes without saying you and your maid should never have come on foot."

"But, sir, I needed the exercise to help deal with my agitation."

"I knew something was amiss. Out with it, child. You'll feel better for sharing it."

"It's Archie, sir. I had to come."

"Lover's quarrel?"

"In a manner of speaking. He wishes to cry off."

"He what?" the earl roared. "Just wait until I see him. He deserves to have his hair combed for causing you a moment's pain."

"Archie broke his word not to gamble. He feels dreadful about letting you down, my lord."

"Never say he sent you to do his dirty-work!" Chandos bellowed.

"No, indeed. I promise you he has no idea I'm here. In fact, he'll probably wring my neck if he ever finds out."

"So if he's got the bottom to tell me to my face, why steal his thunder?"

"Sir, he believes you intend to cast him off. I tried to assure him that we can live comfortably on what my aunt settles on me, but he won't hear of it. His pride won't permit it. So what's to be done?"

The earl reached awkwardly across the tea table to pat Isabella's hunched shoulder with his gnarled, bony hand.

"Don't fret, child. I've no intention of abandoning him. Besides the bargain we struck was twofold. He may have defaulted on the first part, but he did carry through successfully on the second. Which, to my mind, is the more important of the two, if you catch my drift."

"I'm afraid I don't, my lord."

" 'Tis merely that I've decided to make Archie my heir. Thus, he's by no means a pauper even though I'm obliged to cut his allowance for a time as a result of his lapse."

"That's very generous of you, sir. I can't thank you enough."

Chandos impatiently waved her gratitude aside. "Now then," he said with a conspiratorial wink, "suppose you tell me how the lad managed to make a Jack pudding of himself in the first place? Give me the round tale, miss."

"I cannot, sir." Isabella softened her refusal with a rueful grin. "You see, Archie neglected to acquaint me with the particulars."

As usual the library was in a swelter in blithe disregard of the fact that it was a mild June evening. Archie trudged despondently toward his greatuncle, who sat huddled in a chair as close to the blazing fire as possible.

"Upon my soul, you look blue deviled. Sit down before you keel over."

Archie sank into an opposing chair. "I've good reason to be in low spirits. I'd sooner tear out my tongue than cut up your peace but I'm obliged to tell you I've broken my word to you."

"The devil you say! I trust it's not too presumptuous of me to press for details."

"I'd like to oblige you, sir, but first, since it concerns a friend, I need your assurance that nothing I say will go beyond these walls."

"Confound it! I'll have you know I never betray a confidence."

"Forgive me, sir. I meant no offense."

"Well then?"

"I foolishly agreed to accompany Jon Lansbury to a gaming hell he frequents in the hope of checking his excesses."

"I swear if you try to fob me off with some Bambury tale claiming you were lured into play, I'll . . . I'll horsewhip you! You've too much character to let that happen."

Uncomfortably aware of the earl's shrewd gaze, Archie felt a prickly sensation in back of his eyes. If only he had thought things over first, he might have had better sense than to assume Jon's chair at the card table. But he had not taken the time to reason things out. Instead, he had acted on impulse. Now, he must face the consequences.

Archie squared his shoulders. "When Jon staked his diamond stick pin and lost, I forgot all about the bargain you and I struck. All I thought of was winning it back."

"And did you?"

"Of a certainty!" His lips curved in a bittersweet smile. "Suffice to say that the Captain Sharp bent on fleecing Jon failed to achieve his objective."

The earl's black eyes raked his greatnephew's countenance. "I'm sorry to hear you broke your word, but at least there were extenuating circumstances."

"They don't change the fact that I let you down."

"So you did. Ergo, much as I admire your grit for telling me to my face, I must follow through with my threat and cut your allowance for the rest of the year. To be perfectly frank, I don't think you'll be seriously inconvenienced."

"I beg to differ with you, sir. Through my own folly, I've ruined my chance to attach Bella."

"Fiddlestick. Mark my words. She'll raise no dust about making use of her dowry to set up housekeeping."

"What kind of a fribble do you take me for? I'll not sponge off my wife."

"If you don't have a care, you'll break that dear creature's heart because of buffle-headed scruples? Swallow your curst pride and draw on her money whenever you need to for the first year. After that, I'll reinstate your allowance."

"Why should you do that when I didn't adhere to my side of the bargain?"

"Ah, but you did. At least in part."

"I don't understand."

"I swear sometimes I think you were dicked in the nob in your cradle!" exclaimed the irascible old gentleman. "The announcement of your betrothal was printed in the *Gazette*, was it not?"

Archie nodded

"Well there you are! While you inadvertently broke the first part of our bargain, you succeeded with the second when you convinced Isabella Cox to marry you. Thus you are still my heir."

"But, sir, I thought I forfeited that right when I goaded Jon's nemesis into accepting my wager."

"Stubborn, caperwitted noodle! How many times do I have to tell you that *all* you forfeit is your allowance for the balance of the year. Assuming Miss Cox is still of a mind to wed you, you've fulfilled the second part of our bargain and thus stand to inherit my fortune when I cock up my toes."

Archie gave a shaky laugh. "What a mull I've made of things by not paying closer attention to the terms of our agreement."

"Haven't I been saying so till I'm blue in the face?" the earl grumbled.

"To think I was in such despair I tried to get Bella to cry off."

"If I were you, I'd waste no time mending my fences."

"Right, sir. And persuading her to set the date."

"As to that, my doctor recommends I travel to Bath to take the waters. Do you think you can persuade Miss Cox to wait a week or two to be married so I can be present?"

"I doubt she'll have any serious objection, provided I manage to make things right between us." Archie's gray eyes looked troubled. "When do you leave for Bath, sir?"

"Tomorrow morning. Victor has everything in train."

"I'll accompany you, sir."

"Nonsense! I don't need to be mollycoddled. Miss Cox is expecting you to dance attendance upon her at upcoming functions."

"Not until Friday, sir. I can accompany you to Bath and return in plenty of time to escort Bella and her aunt to Carlton House. Besides, my absence will give her temper a chance to cool. Bella was ready to roast me alive when I set her down in Berkeley Square."

Fifteen

Whistling a jaunty tune, Archie clambered down from his godfather's well-sprung berlin, borrowed for the evening so he could escort the ladies to Carlton House in comfort. There was a definite bounce to his step as he mounted the brick steps and lifted the knocker.

"Good evening, sir." The butler took Archie's hat and gloves and deposited them on the hall table.

"Are the ladies down yet, Symonds?"

"No, sir. Perhaps you'd care to await them in the library."

"Excellent."

Ensconced in the bookroom, Archie hoped Bella wasn't still cross with him. He had scarcely had time to scribble her a note explaining he would be away from town for several days as he felt duty bound to escort the earl to Bath, where his elderly relative's doctor had advised him to drink a daily glass of mineral water famed for its curative powers.

His thoughts returned to Bella. What a pity he had no time to patch up their quarrel before they left for Carlton House, but it would not be prudent to leave his uncle's horses standing in the night air. No, much as he desired to set things right between them, he would have to wait for a more propitious moment.

Voices in the hallway brought him to the library's threshold. Archie ran an appreciative eye over the two elegantly attired females. Lady Ponsonby wore a gown of forest green satin, cut daringly low, with an emerald necklace and matching earrings, while Bella looked very fetching in a demure blue silk, with white rosebuds threaded through her elegantly-dressed hair.

So fetching, he could not keep his eyes off her. Lord, but he was a lucky fellow. To think that he had almost whistled the lovely Bella down the wind for the sake of his stiff-necked pride.

"You're in looks tonight, my sweet," Archie murmured as he assisted her into the carriage.

Isabella's speculative glance unsettled him. Little was said as they bowled along cobblestone streets toward the Prince Regent's residence. Archie had no idea why the distaff side of the coach were so quiet, but he for

one was regretting the fact that four days
had passed with no opportunity to clear up
the misunderstanding between Bella and
himself.

Isabella also regretted the time spent apart.
Indeed the four days had seemed like eons.
Happily, Archie appeared to be more his affable self than he had the last time he'd called
on her. The trouble was she had no idea what
his present mood signified. Did it mean he
no longer wished to cry off or not? she wondered.

Frustrated, Isabella stifled a sigh. It would
serve no purpose to quiz him about this admittedly touchy subject en route to Carlton
House. Indeed, should she learn that Archie
stood firm in his resolve to break their engagement, Isabella was not certain she would
not disgrace both herself and her aunt by
bursting into tears. Which would never do.
Aunt Hermione looked forward to an evening at Carlton House and she was determined not to spoil her pleasure.

Seeking for something to take her mind
off her problems, Isabella peeked out the
window and murmured, "So many torches."

"Keep looking, Bella. You'll soon catch a
glimpse of the portico with its imposing
Corinthian pillars."

Noting that Archie had his gaze fixed
upon Carlton House, Isabella seized the
chance to study his profile. What was he

thinking? And what was the outcome of his interview with Chandos?

The interior of Carlton House made quite an impression upon Isabella. Surrounded by regal splendor, she found it amusing to calculate how many ells of draped scarlet silk had been required to adorn the walls of the ballroom.

Leading her into a country dance, Archie asked, "Well, my dear, what do you think of Prinny's palace?"

Isabella considered the high-ceilinged entrance hall lined with columns of porphyry marble, the blue velvet audience room with its elegant velvet settees, the throne room with its rich red brocade and carved painted furnishings, the circular dining room with its mirrored walls. Each room brought new wonders, the ceilings works of art in themselves.

"I'm overwhelmed," she admitted.

Just as they rejoined her aunt on the sidelines, Lady Ponsonby cried, "Amanda, how delicious you look in silver and blue! Have you just arrived? And pray where is . . . oh there you are, Fanny. In primrose, I see. Charming."

Fanny scarcely had time to acknowledge the compliment before a rouge-cheeked young pink, bedecked in shockingly-bright pink satin pantaloons that proclaimed him to

be a tulip of fashion, led her into a quadrille.

Beau Brummell joined the diminished
group. Isabella had always regarded him as
the epitome of sartorial splendor. Her awe
increased as she watched him make an elegant leg to Aunt Hermione.

"The years have treated you kindly. Ever
the Incomparable, my lady."

"Fustian! It's good to see you again,
George."

"Nothing in my style in the wilds of Ireland, I would imagine."

"Nor anywhere else. La, George, surely
you must realize you are an original."

"But of course." He smiled sweetly.
"Prinny sends his compliments. He is desir-
ous of renewing an old acquaintance and
wishful of meeting your niece."

"How kind of him."

"Yes, well it's his birthday and he's in a
magnanimous mood."

"Inform him I shall be pleased to go
along with his wishes. But where are my
manners. George, allow me to make you
known to my niece, Isabella Cox."

"Miss Cox," said Brummell.

Isabella managed a credible curtsy.

"And her fiance, Archibald Brainridge,"
her aunt added.

"Fiance?"

"Fiance," Archie averred firmly— to Isabella's profound relief—once he'd returned Beau Brummell's bow. "I trust his highness has no objection to my coming along?"

A faint frown disturbed Isabella's creamy brow. The hint of steel in Archie's tone bothered her.

Brummell laughed and said in an obviously tongue-in-cheek manner, "My dear fellow, the Regent will be charmed. I confess I can't wait to see his face wreathed in delight."

Lady Ponsonby snapped her fan shut. "La, George, what a whisker! How I've missed your droll sense of humor."

"That's what comes from rusticating in Ireland, my lady." He tucked Lady Ponsonby's arm in his. "Come along, my dears, Prinny don't like to be kept waiting."

Though initially the Prince of Wales regarded Archie with a baleful stare, much of his starchiness wilted when he was informed of their betrothal. And surely, Isabella reasoned, if Archie meant to cry off, he would not dare mislead the Prince Regent.

Prinny chortled. "Stole the march on me, have you, Brainridge? Allow me to compliment you on your good taste. Mind you, Miss Cox doesn't hold a candle to Lady Ponsonby in her prime. Still she's a taking little thing."

"Fie on you, sir!" Lady Ponsonby fluttered

her lashes. "How can you be so cruel as to hint I've lost my looks."

"Never, my dear. I swear you're as lovely as ever."

Isabella was amused by the heightened color in her aunt's cheeks.

"I've made several exquisite additions to my snuff box collection since your last visit. Perhaps you would care to inspect them."

"Lovely!" Hermione agreed.

Prinny beamed.

"Isabella would love to see them, too, wouldn't you, pet?" Hermione amended hastily.

"Above all things, Aunt," Isabella responded, quick to take her aunt's hint since it was common knowledge amongst the *ton* that the Prince Regent had a roving eye and wasn't above making improper advances—given the opportunity.

Thwarted, Prinny's glower was so fierce, Isabella's self confidence faltered. Fortunately for her peace of mind, Beau Brummell's easy laugh provided a welcome diversion.

"Face it, sir, you've been outmaneuvered."

Put on his mettle, the Prince Regent dredged up a smile. "Naughty of you, Hermie, to spoil our *tete-a-tete*. And on my birthday, too."

Lady Ponsonby regarded her sovereign

with cool aplomb. "I'm not quite the innocent I was when you saw me last, sir."

Isabella breathed a little easier. Obviously, her aunt was not the sort to wilt under pressure.

"More's the pity!" Prinny exclaimed feelingly. He gave Archie a cool nod. "Do accompany us, Mr. Brainridge, unless of course a guided tour strikes you as a dead bore."

"Not at all, sire. By all means, lead on."

Noting the dark scowl that Archie addressed to the Prince Regent's back, Isabella experienced a rush of affection. Since they'd lagged behind and thus were unlikely to be overheard, she teased, "You are very protective, sir."

"If you think for a minute I'd let you stroll off in the company of that unprincipled libertine, you're mistaken!"

"Do hush," Isabella cautioned. "He may hear you?"

"Fustian! He's too interested in romancing your aunt to pay me the least mind. Though what you females see in that florid-faced, popeyed, overweight coxcomb is beyond me!"

Isabella smiled. Archie was jealous. Clearly a sign that his affections were fixed. Surely he no longer wished to cry off. But if that was true, why didn't he say so?

They caught up to her aunt and Prinny in

the Chinese drawing room. There, Isabella's interest was captured by a black lacquered screen overprinted with delicately-drawn flowers. Noting her fascination, Prinny graciously explained the process called chinoiserie before steering Lady Ponsonby toward his collection of snuff boxes.

Though intrigued by the screen, Isabella was soon jarred from her reverie by her aunt's soft, startled cry. Catching a sudden flurry of movement from the corner of her eye, she turned her head in time to see mutinous resentment mirrored on Aunt Hermione's flushed face as she adroitly distanced herself from her escort.

The Prince gave a naughty chuckle. When she caught her aunt surreptitiously rubbing her *derriere*, Isabella grinned. Why the sly old roue! He had pinched her aunt. Highly improper, to say the least.

Back in the ballroom, Isabella was obliged to hide a smirk behind her fan when Prinny's stays creaked as he made a final bow to a definitely out-of-sorts Hermione. Grandison intercepted the prince after he took his leave. Just out of earshot, they exchanged a few jovial remarks before continuing on their separate ways.

Hermione's expression softened when Grandison halted before her. Indeed, he even coaxed a smile from her as he led her onto the dance floor.

Much later, driving toward Berkeley Square in Chandos's carriage, Isabella regretted that she and Archie had had no chance to talk all evening. The berlin rolled to a stop in front of her aunt's town house. No doubt, it was too late to invite him in for a private conversation. Isabella sighed. Aunt Hermione would be scandalized if she even made such a bizarre suggestion.

After helping her alight, Archie squeezed Isabella's hand and said in a soft undertone, "We must settle things between us. I'll call on you tomorrow."

Tomorrow? How cruel to make her wait another day to learn his true sentiments. Surely if he loved her, he would have found a moment during the evening to put her out of her misery. Isabella lifted her chin. She had no choice but to agree, but by heaven if Archie didn't make things right between them tomorrow, she would fling his betrothal ring back in his face!

The following morning, Symonds materialized in the archway leading into a small sitting room. "Begging your pardon, miss."

Reluctantly Isabella raised her eyes from a romance novel she'd secured at Hookham's Library on Fanny's recommendation. "Yes, what is it?"

The butler mopped his florid brow with a linen handkerchief. "I'm caught at point-non-plus. Lady Lansbury desires to speak to Lady Ponsonby on a matter of extreme urgency, but Elsbeth sent down word that her ladyship is indisposed."

"Very well, Symonds. I'll have a word with Lady Lansbury in my aunt's stead."

"Very good, miss."

With a sigh, Isabella closed the book. She'd intended to laze about the house today, doing nothing more strenuous than reading one of Mrs. Radcliffe's novels. However, the matter must be very pressing to bring Lady Lansbury to Berkeley Square at such an unfashionable hour.

Isabella swept into the drawing room. Lady Lansbury's eyes darted in her direction, then dropped away in obvious disappointment.

"My lady, my aunt is not receiving callers. Will I do?"

Her ladyship burst into tears. Astonished, Isabella tried to calm the distraught woman. "What's overset you, ma'am? Fanny's not in some scrape, I trust?"

"Fanny? Indeed not! Nor is Jon, thanks to Mr. Brainridge— who not only rescued him from that gaming hell— but won back the diamond stick pin he foolishly wagered."

A soft smile touched Isabella's lips. So that's why Archie had gambled. Trust him to risk all for someone he cared about. No wonder she loved him.

"But I stray from the purpose of my visit." Lady Lansbury dabbed her cheeks with a lace-edged square of Irish linen, then took Isabella's hand and patted it distractedly.

"You're almost as dear to me as my own daughter! Such a shame to spoil your chances." She released Isabella's hand to daintily wipe her nose. "I must go, my dear." She stuffed her handkerchief back in her reticule and rose.

"Go. But, ma'am, you haven't told me why you came?"

"Your aunt will explain. She must. It is unfair to keep you in the dark." At the threshold, she wheeled around suddenly. "Hermie should never have gone to Carlton House. The tattlemongers will pounce on her latest indiscretion as a pretext to air the old rumors surrounding her banishment to Ireland. Good day, my dear. Do try not to be too hard on your aunt. There's a good girl!" On a flood of fresh sobs, Lady Lansbury floated from the room.

Isabella retired to a chair, totally at a loss to understand Lady Lansbury's disjointed conversation. For that matter, what had induced her aunt to turn away her dearest friend? The only way to get to the crux of the matter was to march upstairs and demand an explanation. Yet, Isabella was reluctant to do so. She had a sinking feeling that Lady Lansbury was alluding to her aunt's deplorable tendency, but prayed she was mistaken.

While she attempted to pluck up sufficient courage to confront her aunt, Elsbeth entered.

"May I have a word with you, miss?"

"Certainly."

Wringing her hands, Elsbeth said, "Last night, her ladyship returned from Carlton House in a high fidget. I had to resort to ten drops of laudanum, before she finally fell asleep."

Isabella sighed. "Stop trying to soften the blow. What took her fancy this time?"

The abigail slipped a hand into her apron pocket and drew out something small enough to fit within her closed fist which she thrust toward Isabella. "Here, take it! I want no part of it."

"What is it?"

Elsbeth slowly opened her palm.

"Angels defend us! It's one of Prinny's snuff boxes! But when did she have the chance?" Isabella asked, genuinely bewildered. "I was with her every minute."

"Don't blame yourself, miss. She's a sly one. She's even fooled me a time or two and, believe me, I'm always on the lookout. Usually what she takes is of little value, but sometimes what catches her eye is very dear."

"As the Prince Regent's snuff box undoubtedly is."

"Yes, miss." Elsbeth's thin shoulders sagged. "What's to be done? My lady's too gentle-bred for Newgate."

"Would the courts of justice actually deal with her so harshly?"

The abigail shrugged. "Mayhap, they'd send her to Bedlam instead."

"The insane asylum? God save her!" Isabella cried. "At all costs I must prevent that. Even if it means I must try and return the prince's snuff box myself."

"Surely, miss, it would be wiser to request your betrothed's help as we did on a previous occasion."

Isabella shook her head. "Much as it grieves me to admit it, I fear his regard for me may not be as steady as I once believed. No, Elsbeth, I must undertake this on my own. Fetch my pelisse."

Alone in the drawing room, Isabella examined the snuff box more closely. Painstakingly enameled by hand, its workmanship was exquisite. "Such a small thing to cause such a fuss!" she said in an awed whisper.

"I took the liberty of ordering the carriage," the abigail said as she helped Isabella don her pelisse.

"Cancel it. Can you imagine the field day the tattlemongers will enjoy, should they espy the Ponsonby barouche in front of Carlton

House?" Isabella dropped the snuff box into one of the pelisse's deep pockets. "No, Elsbeth, I must go by hack."

Sixteen

At Carlton House, Isabella's hand shook so badly she had difficulty raising the ornate knocker. The door widened revealing a dimly-lit interior. She stiffened watery knees and stepped inside.

The major domo looked her up and down and cocked his head quizzically. She swallowed in a vain effort to soothe her scratchy throat.

"I . . . I need to see the Prince Regent on a private matter."

"Do you have an appointment?"

Isabella shook her head.

"This is highly irregular, miss. His highness rarely emerges from his private suite before noon."

Isabella mentally dug in her heels. "I dislike being a nuisance but the matter is urgent."

In the face of her persistence, the major domo requested her name and bade her wait on a bench in the anteroom. Then, shaking his head as if at the follies of youth, he exited.

If that was truly what he thought, Isabella was inclined to agree with him. Yet, her aunt's future happiness rested solely on the success of her mission. Her nerves were stretched taut by the time the major domo reappeared with a gentleman he introduced as the Prince Regent's private secretary, Mr. Herbert Taylor.

Taylor regarded Isabella with the zeal of a scientist studying a mounted specimen. "The prince sends his compliments. He will honor your request for an audience. If you will follow me, Miss Cox."

A sense of foreboding gripped her. It intensified with each step she took. But although sorely tempted to show the white feather, the thought of Aunt Hermione moldering away in either Newgate or Bedlam checked Isabella's impulse to flee. Instead, she stiffened her spine, and ever mindful of the delicacy of her errand, followed the secretary's lead. Isabella recognized the Chinese drawing room the instant she crossed the threshold. Taylor announced her, bowed to the prince and quit the room.

Prinny sat slouched in a wing chair large enough to accommodate his immense girth. His rotund figure encased in a paisley print silk dressing gown, an indulgent smile lit his florid countenance as Isabella arose from her obligatory curtsy. As he lifted her hand to his lips, Isabella noted the puffiness of facial tissues and the dark pouches beneath protuberant blue eyes with swiftly-veiled distaste.

Until that instant, she had done her best to ignore rumors alluding to the prince's decadent life. But now, studying his haggard appearance, she decided they more than likely contained a grain of truth. Indeed, one of the more shocking tales came to mind. Apparently Prinny and his brothers, the royal dukes, had challenged each other as to which of them could consume the most bottles of port at a single sitting. The Duke of York won. He drank thirty-three consecutive bottles of wine before joining his brothers, who'd already drunk themselves into a stupor.

Isabella was recalled from her musings by the creak of Prinny's stays as he tottered to his feet.

"My dear, what a pleasant surprise."

"Thank you, sir, for receiving me at such an inopportune hour."

"Not at all. How may I serve you?"

"Actually, I'd like another peek at your snuff boxes, if it won't put you to too much trouble."

"Entirely at your service, my dear." He tucked her arm in his and led her toward a long table where the small boxes were attractively displayed. With a lazy wave, he indicated the glass cabinet. "The rest of the collection's in there."

She made a swift, keen-eyed study of the snuff boxes, her gaze faltering when she discovered a gap in their ranks. Her heartbeat accelerated and her pulses began to throb. *Almost certainly the snuff box in her pocket belonged in that exact spot!*

"Fancy a closer look at those in the glass cabinet?" He held up a key.

"That would be splendid."

Wheezing from his exertions, Prinny jiggled the key in the brass lock, attempting to get it properly seated so it would turn. Taking advantage of his preoccupation, Isabella carefully drew the purloined snuff box from her pocket and returned it to its rightful place. Quite suddenly, Prinny whirled around to face her.

Isabella gave a guilty start. *Thank goodness her hand no longer touched the snuff box!*

But her short-lived complacency vanished the instant she saw cold fury in Prinny's faded blue eyes.

"So Hermione expects to escape her fate once again?" Petulant lips curled in a jaded smile. "At least you're an improvement over her last emissary."

"Emissary? I don't understand."

"It's quite simple. I let you return my snuff box to its customary resting place, but I'm aware of your aunt's weakness. You see, this is the second time she's prigged one of my snuff boxes. Last time, her husband interceded. In exchange for scotching the scandal, he agreed to persuade her ladyship to retire permanently from society. This time, however, Hermione has no protector."

Isabella lifted her chin. "On the contrary, sir. I am her protector."

"A mere female? Pray don't be nonsensical."

Taking umbrage, she informed him tartly, "Your Highness, I'm just as capable as my uncle of convincing my aunt a return to her Irish estate is in her best interest."

"Ah, but this time I don't intend to let Hermione off so lightly. I intend to claim her favors in exchange for my silence."

"Shame on you, sir."

"My dear Miss Cox, has anyone ever told you how beautiful you are when angry?" He seized her hand, gazing at her with such an odd smile, it occasioned an involuntary shiver.

Glaring, she said, "Release me, sir."

"By thunder, I won't. I would have preferred that Hermione come herself, but you'll do in her stead."

Though his mouth curved in a smile, the expression in his eyes was hard. Chills of terror shot through her. God save her! Prince or no, she appeared to be in the clutches of an aging lecher. Isabella yanked her hand from his grasp and began to back away. Moving with more agility than she believed him to possess, Prinny reached the room's threshold first, effectively blocking off her escape.

Isabella shuddered. She wouldn't give in to him! She would not! Though how in the world she'd manage to outwit him was unfortunately not clear.

Rigged out in a new pearl-gray superfine coat by Weston, snowy neckcloth arranged to perfection by his valet, with pale yellow pantaloons and polished Hessians, Archie stood poised on the doorstep of the Ponsonby town house.

When the door opened, he stepped inside. "I know I am shockingly early, Symonds. I promise to wait quietly until the ladies are ready to receive a morning caller."

"I regret that's impossible, sir. Her ladyship is indisposed and Miss Isabella has gone out. Perhaps you would care to leave your card."

"Gone out? So early? And Lady Ponsonby? Not ill, I trust."

"Indeed, it is not my place to say. If you will leave your—"

"The devil with my card! Something haveycavey's afoot and I mean to get to the bottom of it. Step aside!"

In icy tones, the butler stated, "Sir, I know my duty. I must ask you to leave at once!"

"Wait!" cried a female voice from the upper landing. Turning, the staid butler eyed Elsbeth with distaste.

"It's imperative that I speak to Mr. Brainridge. Show him into the morning room."

Attacked on two fronts, Symonds capitulated. He ushered Archie into the room designated by the abigail.

In the morning room, Archie smiled coaxingly at Elsbeth. "Suppose you tell me what's put you in a high fidget."

"Something dreadful has happened, sir. Miss Isabella went to try and put things right. She's been gone the better part of an hour and I fear I'm in danger of having a nervous spasm."

"Calm yourself. How can I help?"

"I'm so glad you've come, Mr. Brainridge. I suggested Miss Isabella apply to you to put things right as you did on a previous occasion. However, she seemed to think you no longer cared for her."

Archie winced. He had felt he was doing the honorable thing by suggesting Bella cry off. Only now did he fully realize how deeply he had hurt her.

"I see. Where was she bound?"

"To Carlton House to return a snuff box."

Archie paled. Obviously Lady Ponsonby was up to her old tricks. "Good God!"

Elsbeth wrung her hands. "I do wish she hadn't insisted upon a hackney."

"Yes, well Bella's headstrong, but don't worry. I'm off to rescue her from the scrape she's embroiled in!"

Archie raced out of the town house and scrambled up into the high seat of his phaeton. As the team jogged along at a fast clip, his forehead furrowed until it resembled a freshly-plowed field. It had not been his intention to set foot in Berkeley Square until afternoon, but he had awakened quite early beset by vague fears concerning his betrothed. Finally he had grown so uneasy that he had called Percy to help him dress. He had arrived at the Ponsonby town house shortly before eleven o'clock.

Good thing too! For Bella could be in serious trouble. How could she have been so hen-witted as to go to Carlton House alone? Prince of the realm or no, if that aging rake dared . . .

Archie forced himself to draw a deep breath. No use working himself into a rage. He must keep a cool head if he meant to rescue Bella.

A quarter of an hour later, he climbed out of his phaeton and shouted to his tiger to walk the horses but not to stray too far from the entrance of Carlton House as they might have to leave in a hurry. Bounding up the steps, he pounded on the door.

* * *

Isabella was tired. Tired of playing cat and mouse. Tired of trying to grapple with her aunt's problem. Tired of trying to hatch a brilliant scheme that would free her from certain ruin.

The Chinese drawing room had long since lost its charm in her eyes. Indeed, it had taken on the chilling aura of an intricate web— complete with a bug-eyed, obese spider stealthily sidling closer and closer.

Whatever was she going to do? Surely there was a way out of this coil— if only she could think of it. Frantically, she wracked her brain, seeking a solution. Initially she drew a blank but, just when she was about to give up the fight, a germ of an idea sprouted. Praying she had guessed right, she no longer took pains to hide the profound sadness she felt at the prospect of her eminent loss of innocence.

The instantaneous change in the Regent's demeanor from hardened roue to a mischievous charmer stunned Isabella.

"My dear Miss Cox, I wish you would not regard me as a noxious potion you are obliged to swallow."

Could Prinny's conscience be plaguing him? Isabella wondered. Determined to play what she perceived as a chink in his armor for all it was worth, she observed, "The person I pity is not myself, sir, but my poor aunt."

Prinny peered at her quizzically. "Lady Ponsonby? In heaven's name why?"

"I fear she's about to suffer a grave disillusionment. In her eyes, no one has a higher sense of honor than you do, sir. Indeed, she regards you as the first Gentleman of Europe and holds you in the highest esteem."

"Does she, by jove? Well bless my soul."

Observing the rapid display of warring emotions that darted across the royal countenance, Isabella felt almost as if she were seeing the cogs of Prinny's mind spinning as he grappled with his dilemma. Not only was his personal honor at stake, to ravish Lady Ponsonby's niece meant losing her ladyship's good opinion of him forevermore.

Prince Regent shot Isabella a beatific smile calculated to disarm the most wary female. "Pray be seated, Miss Cox. We must talk."

Grandison was about to leave his rented suite of rooms in Ryder Street when an undernourished lad delivered Lady Ponsonby's distraught note. Unable to make head nor tails of the contents, he rushed to Berkeley Square.

The instant he was ushered into Hermione's presence, she exclaimed, "Thank God, you've come!"

"You're lucky your potboy caught me at home." His smile faded when he saw her tear-stained face. "My dear, what's amiss?"

"I feel wretched. Isabella's in danger and it's my fault. You see I . . ." Hermione's cheeks tinged a delicate pink. "I've a deplorable habit of appropriating things that capture my fancy."

"Yes, my love, I know."

Hermione stared at him from startled green eyes. "You do? How long have you known?"

"For eons?"

"Eons," she echoed.

He laughed. "Why do you suppose I was so adamantly opposed to your going to London? You're safer residing at your country estate. The folks thereabouts are too fond of you to make a fuss."

"How did you find out?"

Grandison's eyes twinkled. "Dearest, this is not the first time you prigged my watch. On the previous occasion, Robert returned it to me and confided that he compensated a steady stream of local tradesmen whenever you indulged in a shopping binge."

Hermione's face flushed crimson. Desiring to put her at ease, he said, "But the past is over and done with. If you wish me to rescue your niece, I need more details."

Obviously agitated, Hermione bit her lower lip. "Last night, I stole one of Prinny's snuff-boxes. This morning while I slept Isabella took it upon herself to return it. She's been gone far too long. I'm desperately worried. Will you help me?"

Grandison's tender gaze did not waver. "My dearest love, your wish is my command."

"You will be careful?"

He read genuine concern in Hermione's gaze. The tension in his shoulders relaxed. Saints be praised! She cared.

Having learned from the major domo that his royal highness was entertaining Miss Cox in the Chinese drawing room, Archie brushed aside the timid servant and strode purposely down the corridor.

Pausing at the room's entrance, he exclaimed, "Isabella!"

Isabella was so startled she almost dropped the delicate China teacup.

"Archie! Is it truly you?"

"Bella, dearest, are you all right?"

Prinny feigned a yawn. "Dear me! However did you manage to elude the house guard? Mr. Brainridge, if my memory hasn't played me false."

Archie's fists clenched. How dare he entertain Bella unchaperoned! Of course, it would never do to plant the Prince Regent a facer, but by heaven he was tempted!

"Correct, sir. Perhaps you will also recall that Isabella's my intended."

Prinny gave a rueful chuckle. "Rest assured, your betrothed never let me forget that fact for a minute. I trust you appreciate your good fortune. Your chosen bride is a rare treasure."

Relaxing tense muscles, Archie flushed with pleasure. "That's quite a compliment, sir. Thank you."

Prinny gave a negligent shrug. "As you see, Miss Cox and I are enjoying a light repast. Will you join us, Mr. Brainridge?"

"Some other time, your highness. I've come to escort Bella home, with your permission, of course."

Prinny's demeanor took on the mulish cast of a spoiled child denied his favorite toy. Isabella's jawbone clenched. But even as she steeled herself in anticipation of impending disaster, Malcolm Grandison spoke from the room's threshold.

"Forgive the intrusion, your highness, but I think it would be wise to accede to the young man's request." Advancing with confidence, the Irishman wagged a finger at the Prince Regent. "Detaining innocent maidens is not your usual style, is it, sir?"

Prinny bristled. "Damn your eyes, Grandison! Just because you and I have had dealings in the past doesn't give you the right to stick your nose in my business."

"Hermione Ponsonby *is* my business, sir. I'm trustee of her estate. And as Miss Cox is her niece, naturally I take a fatherly interest in her welfare as well."

"There was no need for either you or Mr. Brainridge to come dashing to the rescue," Prinny said pettishly. "Why I wouldn't dream of harming a hair on Miss Cox's head."

Grandison trained his gaze upon Archie and Bella and jerked his head toward the door. "Off with you, brats."

Archie hesitated. "What of you, sir?"

Grandison indulged in a hearty laugh. "Don't worry about me, Brainridge. I usually land on my feet. Get your betrothed out of here before her reputation ends up in shreds."

He prodded Archie and Isabella toward the room's archway— all the time ignoring Prinny's sputter of indignation. At the threshold, he gave them each a firm shove. "Get going. I'll be along in a thrice. Just need a minute to soothe my liege's ruffled feathers."

Archie paused in the hallway. "Grandison, I cannot tell you how much we appreciate— "

"Stubble it, lad. If Hermione hadn't told me what was afoot, I've not a doubt in the world that you'd have managed to rescue Bella entirely on your own. Besides my motive is self serving. I've reason to hope that Hermie will be so impressed with my timely intervention, she will finally allow herself to be persuaded to marry me." Grandison winked. "Now make yourselves scarce."

Bowling along in the high perch phaeton with yellow wheels, Isabella's nose remained slightly out of joint. While grateful to both her would-be saviors, the fact remained that she'd rescued herself. What rankled was that she'd received no credit for her ingenuity. On the other hand, considering the fragility of the male ego, perhaps it would be wise to keep her tongue between her teeth.

Isabella stole a glance at Archie in an effort to divine his present frame of mind. Catching her at it, he demanded, "What mischief are you planning now, you troublesome baggage?"

"None. I swear it! I was just thinking how handsome you look in your finery."

"Special occasion," he admitted gruffly as he pulled the chestnuts to a halt in front of her aunt's town house.

"Oh?" Isabella turned to face him.

Archie grinned. "Thought it about time I ask you to set the date for our wedding."

"Really? I collect that the last time we talked, you wished me to cry off."

"I thought it was the proper thing to do under the circumstances. Of course, that was before Chandos set me straight. Turns out I misunderstood our bargain. I'm still his heir, provided you'll have me, sweetheart."

"How can you doubt it? After all, I'm the one who refused to cry off."

"Thank God one of us don't want for sense. Come closer, my love. I mean to kiss you breathless."

Isabella fluttered her lashes flirtatiously. "In an open carriage? How shocking!"

"Come here, you wretch, before I give in to the temptation to ravish you on the spot!"

"Very well, sir. I've no wish to create a scandal."

Isabella nestled obligingly against Archie's broad chest and lifted her face in anticipation of his kiss.

"Happy, Bella?"

"Yes. And you?"

"Happy as a grig, my dearest love," he assured her just before he kissed her.

TODAY'S HOTTEST READS
ARE TOMORROW'S SUPERSTARS

VICTORY'S WOMAN   (4484, $4.50)
by Gretchen Genet
Andrew — the carefree soldier who sought glory on the battlefield, and returned a shattered man . . . Niall — the legandary frontiersman and a former Shawnee captive, tormented by his past . . . Roger — the troubled youth, who would rise up to claim a shocking legacy . . . and Clarice — the passionate beauty bound by one man, and hopelessly in love with another. Set against the backdrop of the American revolution, three men fight for their heritage — and one woman is destined to change all their lives forever!

FORBIDDEN   (4488, $4.99)
by Jo Beverley
While fleeing from her brothers, who are attempting to sell her into a loveless marriage, Serena Riverton accepts a carriage ride from a stranger — who is the handsomest man she has ever seen. Lord Middlethorpe, himself, is actually contemplating marriage to a dull daughter of the aristocracy, when he encounters the breathtaking Serena. She arouses him as no woman ever has. And after a night of thrilling intimacy — a forbidden liaison — Serena must choose between a lady's place and a woman's passion!

WINDS OF DESTINY   (4489, $4.99)
by Victoria Thompson
Becky Tate is a half-breed outcast — branded by her Comanche heritage. Then she meets a rugged stranger who awakens her heart to the magic and mystery of passion. Hiding a desperate past, Texas Ranger Clint Masterson has ridden into cattle country to bring peace to a divided land. But a greater battle rages inside him when he dares to desire the beautiful Becky!

WILDEST HEART   (4456, $4.99)
by Virginia Brown
Maggie Malone had come to cattle country to forge her future as a healer. Now she was faced by Devon Conrad, an outlaw wounded body and soul by his shadowy past . . . whose eyes blazed with fury even as his burning caress sent her spiraling with desire. They came together in a Texas town about to explode in sin and scandal. Danger was their destiny — and there was nothing they wouldn't dare for love!

Available wherever paperbacks are sold, or order direct from the Publisher. Send cover price plus 50¢ per copy for mailing and handling to Penguin USA, P.O. Box 999, c/o Dept. 17109, Bergenfield, NJ 07621. Residents of New York and Tennessee must include sales tax. DO NOT SEND CASH.